THE GREAT AMERICAN BETRAYAL

SCOTT STEIN

TinyFox
PRESS

A Tiny Fox Press Book

Library of Congress Control Number: 2022930683

ISBN: 978-1-946501-45-5

Tiny Fox Press and the book fox logo are all registered trademarks of Tiny Fox Press LLC

Tiny Fox Press LLC
North Port, Florida

"*The Great American Betrayal* is a wickedly funny novel jam-packed with madcap invention and verbal hijinks that are **sure to be a hit with fans of Douglas Adams and Stanislaw Lem**. Scott Stein writes wild plots and sentences that tie your brain in delicious knots while working his inimitable brand of bravura cosmic absurdity. God bless him."

— Gabe Hudson, author of *Dear Mr. President* and *Gork, the Teenage Dragon*

"**Delightful, sparkling, zany, with clever references to Kafka and Orwell and Borges**, and narrated by a lovable crime-solving coffeebot, *The Great American Betrayal* takes the dysfunction of our social-media-riveted world **and ramps it up to absurdist heights in service of a rollicking, engrossing mystery**."

— Vikram Paralkar, author of *Night Theater* and *The Afflictions*

"**I love Scott Stein's writing.** It's effervescent. *The Great American Betrayal* practically fizzed on my tongue. **It's sharp and silly and a hell of a lot of fun to read**."

— Mike Sacks, author of *Passing on the Right, Stinker Lets Loose,* and *Poking a Dead Frog*

"**Stein's *The Great American Betrayal* is a blast!** A coffee-maker turned detective and his laconic, 'Not-An-English-Professor' partner deliver a fun story and a good-humored skewering of contemporary American culture in this winning sequel."

— Chantel Acevedo, author of the *Muse Squad* series and *The Curse on Spectacle Key*

ALSO BY SCOTT STEIN

The Great American Deception
Mean Martin Manning
Lost

For Griffin

"Et tu, Brute?"
Julius Caesar[1] (Act III, Scene I). William Shakespeare[2]

---

[1] It isn't certain that Caesar ever said these words. Not only that, but he never tasted the salad dressing that bears his name, and possibly didn't even like croutons.

[2] Unless someone other than Shakespeare wrote Shakespeare's plays, which is a matter of great controversy to approximately six people.

Our second case was a real humdinger, which everyone knows is the most challenging variety of dinger. Maybe I'll tell you about it some time, if you have the required security clearance. Right now, however, I'm telling you the story of our third case. It might not have been a humdinger, but it more than made up for that by being a real can of worms.

If this doesn't impress you, it could be that you don't realize just how challenging a can of worms is. Perhaps you assume worms are easy to manage because, as invertebrates, they're generally spineless. You might be thinking, *Nothing to worry about here, just a can of worms*. You might even be saying to anyone who happens to be passing by, "Have no fear, a can of worms is actually pretty easy to handle. It's just worms in a can, after all."[3] And maybe, just maybe, you could be right that a can of worms is really no trouble, but of course that's assuming you kept the lid closed.

"Arjay, what did you do?" famous private detective Frank Harken[4] asked. "Did you take the lid off the can of worms?"

"Yes," I said. It was true. If you're wondering why I had a can of worms in the first place, if you're imagining I'm some kind of insane bot who carries around a can of worms everywhere for no reason at all, you can rest easy. I had a very good reason for carrying a can of worms. We were fishing. Yes, for fish. It was our first time visiting the Great American Lake. It wasn't a naturally occurring body of water—you'd call it a humanmade lake if humans had made it, but they hadn't. As always, many years earlier, bots had done the heavy lifting[5] while people pointed at what they wanted done and where. The lake was twelve acres and shaped like a kidney, which was one of the most popular shapes for a lake. It was encircled[6] by a smooth walking path and enough synthetic grass for people to spread out blankets and enjoy a lovely lakeview picnic. The ceiling didn't look like a ceiling. In the Great American, they often didn't. Projectors and screens created the illusion of drifting cumulus clouds, puffy white against the blue sky above and all around to the treeline on the distant high walls. It was a beautiful spring day at the lake, like every other day of the year.

The rowbot on the floor in the center of our canoe was a squat rectangular chap with two long flexible oarms. One oarm alternated paddling on either side of the boat to propel us

---

[3] And they might be wondering what you're talking about, especially if they're carrying a can of not-worms, or a jar, or nothing at all.

[4] You've probably heard of him, because that's what *famous* means. If you haven't, don't worry—you can learn all about him in my chronicle of our first case, *The Great American Deception*. However, if you decide to read about it, be warned that even though it wasn't a humdinger, it was quite a doozy.

[5] In this case, the heavy lifting was mostly digging.

[6] *Enkidneyed* would be more precise, but that isn't a word.

through the water; the other oarm stretched back to the rear of the canoe and steered. The canoe was a simulated western red cedar dugout, a perfect plastic wood replica that had an official stamp of authenticity on its side. When the rowbot ceased paddling, we glided another 45.72 feet and came to a rest. A floating breezebot breezed us at a relaxing, moderate setting.

Unfortunately, despite the breeze, Frank Harken was not doing a good job of relaxing. "This is complete chaos—our worms are everywhere!"

This was not literally true. At most, it was partial chaos—there were plenty of places our worms were not. Most places, really. But indeed a few worms had wormed their way to the front of the canoe and others were worming toward the back. So, if it wasn't exactly complete chaos, it wasn't quite perfect order, either.

"Arjay, why'd you take the lid off?"

"I had never met worms before. It seemed only polite to introduce myself."

"Worms don't do introductions," Harken said.

He was right. Rudely, the worms had not said hello nor offered to shake any of my four hands before wriggling every which way out of the can and all around the canoe.

"What are we even doing here, at the lake, of all places?"[7] Harken asked.

"We're fishing," I reminded him. "It's generally preferable to do that near a body of water."

"I know we're fishing." He held up the fishing rod as evidence, in case I'd forgotten that he was a detective. "Why are we fishing?"

"We already talked about this. It's our eight-day-iversary and we're at the Great American Lake to celebrate and get some

---

[7] Not to be confused with The Lake of All Places, a water amusement restaurant that could simulate any known location. For example, molk (mall folk) could eat dinner while seeming to cruise across Lake Eerie, Lake Tahoe, Lake Superior, or even through the canals of Venice, New York, or Mars, among many other choices.

well-deserved relaxation. I asked you what you did to relax on the outside, and you said you used to fish when you were a boy. So here we are."

"Here we are. And I said I went fishing a couple of times, not that I *used to fish*."

"I'm not seeing a distinction." It's true. I wasn't.

"You badgered me for days to tell you about my childhood outside. 'I want more backstory,' you said. And to get you to give me a moment of peace, I told you about how my father took me to the reservoir they kept stocked with bass, and we fished there. I told you he took me exactly twice, that we caught nothing at all, that it didn't matter anyway because the bass probably weren't safe to eat. Both times, my father didn't say a word to me the whole day. It wasn't some magical bonding experience. I barely remembered it. Somehow you heard all that and concluded that this would be relaxing for me. I swear, this is the last time I let your incessant badgering[8] push me to do something I don't want to do."

Just then a rainbow trout leapt from the lake and landed in our boat. It flopped around a bit, like a fish out of water, which is an expression but also exactly what it was.

"Good job, Frank Harken. You've caught another one." It was the eleventh trout to jump into our boat. I had set the fishing level to easy.

"This isn't fishing!" Harken said. "Fish aren't supposed to leap at you. Arjay, I've humored you long enough today. First of all, *eight-day-iversary* isn't a thing—"

I stopped him right there. "—It very much is a thing. In the Great American, 68.3% of new couples celebrate their eight-day-iversary. Furthermore, all versaries are a thing if you believe in

---

[8] It was his second mention of badgers even though that species was not known for lake-dwelling and we hadn't seen any at the Great American Lake. We had seen a family of beavers building a dam by a small inlet that led to a filtration system. They were not badgers despite having the same number of syllables and letters and some letters in common. Frank Harken was not much of a taxonomist.

them. In fifteen more days it will be our twenty-three-day-iversary, and we'll celebrate that as well. The beginning of a partnership as great as ours should be commemorated as often as possible."

Harken looked at me and slowly shook his head. "I wasn't done talking. That's why I started with *First of all.*"

I conceded that this was a valid point. "I would be happy to hear your second of all."

He didn't seem to have a second-of-all in mind, hesitated, then found one. "Second of all, we are not a new couple."

"Frank Harken, I know math is not your specialty, but I believe you do know that there are two of us. That's what *a couple* means. And we've only known each other for eight days, which makes us new. Hence, we're a new couple."

"You're being too literal. *New couple* implies a romantic relationship. You know, the kind that usually involves two members of the same species, and not a man and an appliance. You do understand we don't have a romantic relationship, right?"

"Of course I know that," I said, a little insulted that Harken had the temerity to think he was my type. "We're partners. But we can still celebrate our eight-day-iversary. Speaking of which, I got you something."

"What do you mean?"

It was a strange question. What could it mean besides my having got him something? "I mean I got you something."

I held out a wrapped box with a bow on top.

"What's this?"

"It's a wrapped box with a bow on top. It's a gift."

"I can see that," Harken said. "What's in it?"

"That's not how opening gifts works. There's supposed to be the element of surprise. That's why it's wrapped. You have to unwrap it to find out what's in it."

Harken might have been losing patience with me, which I gleaned from his shaking head and his clear articulation of the words, "I'm losing patience with you." We would never have a relaxing eight-day-iversary at the lake with the mood he was in.

I handed him a cup of coffee.[9] As always, he received the life-affirming beverage with gratitude and took a sip. And as always, sipping the coffee helped Harken find some of the patience he was losing. He accepted the wrapped box with a bow on top and began the arduous task of removing the striped wrapping paper—I was a thorough gift wrapper, but after one minute and twelve seconds of determined ripping, he succeeded in getting to the box and opening it.

"It's a hat." He was quite perceptive. "Why would I need a hat in the Great American? There's no sun or rain, no weather at all in most locations."

"This isn't just any hat," I said. "It's a fedora."

"I don't see why the kind of hat matters. I still don't need one."

"Frank Harken, you're a private detective. You should wear a hat."

"Detectives don't have to wear hats."

"They don't have to, but the best detectives do. For example, Sherlock Holmes, perhaps the greatest detective of all, was known for wearing a deerstalker. However, since we're not in the woods very often and even when we are there's little chance we'll be stalking deer, that didn't seem like the best choice of hat. A fedora, though, is always in fashion, and some truly great detectives are known for wearing one."

"Please don't list all the detectives who wore fedoras."

"I won't. There are some great ones, of course, like Sam Spade and Dick Tracy. But the fedora has also enhanced the heads of such famous non-detective adventurers as Indiana Jones[10] and Leonard Cohen."

---

[9] This might be a good time to tell you that I'm a coffeemaker. If you already know this because you've read *The Great American Deception*, feel free to ignore this footnote. Use the extra time to do whatever you want. Maybe have a cup of coffee.

[10] A fictional archaeologist who hated snakes, Nazis, and anything resembling actual archaeology.

"I know the songwriter but haven't heard of the others. Anyway, I'm not wearing a hat. And don't argue with me—it isn't up for discussion."

Frank Harken could be quite stubborn. I had expected as much, which is why I'd purchased a hat that fit *me*.[11] "Well, I can see there's no use trying to persuade you." And I placed the fedora on my own rounded top—you might call it a head if you insisted that this is where hats had to be worn, though my top didn't look like a head or contain components found in most heads.

"Arjay, what are you doing?"

"I'm wearing a hat."

"You look ridiculous. Coffeemakers don't wear hats."

"Ah, but I'm not just a coffeemaker. I'm also a detective. A detective-in-training, at least."

"You still look ridiculous. But I know how stubborn you can be. You want to wear a hat, wear a hat."

"I will," I said, and I did.

Harken was still shaking his head with disapproval at my hat when something caught his eye[12] in the distance. "Arjay, how long has that man been looking at us?"

"The man wearing the military uniform in the red rowboat? The one staring in this direction?"

"Yes."

"Four minutes and twenty-eight seconds, with only two breaks, of five and nine seconds, respectively."

"Were you planning to tell me he was looking at us?"

"No. I assumed he was just admiring my hat." It was clear a moment later this assumption was incorrect.

---

[11] A classic Homer Simpson gift-giving tactic. See *The Simpsons* episode "Life on the Fast Lane" (1990). Or don't. I'm not the boss of you.

[12] Fortunately, not literally, because we were fishing and a hook catching an eye would be unpleasant at best.

Its rowbot stroking oars deep and steady, the rowboat conveyed the man in the uniform closer to our canoe. As his boat drew alongside us, we could see that his uniform was festooned with seventeen medals, none of which corresponded to any military in the history of the world. They dangled from colorful ribbons and were shiny just like me. Also dangling but less shiny were the man's jowls, which, like the rest of his flesh, were the color and texture of low-fat cottage cheese that had been left out too long. It was impossible to know his age by looking at him—facial alteration was common in the Great American and usually aesthetically successful, but if taken too far could sometimes leave people resembling a collection of vaguely organic lumps. If I had to guess, I would have said he was a few years older than Harken. Fortunately, age-guessing was not compulsory. His eyes were close-set and dark, his luxurious, shiny black hair smoothed back with some kind of gelatinous concoction composed of exotic ingredients that defied precise analysis at this distance. I'd have to get a strand for testing.

"Detective Frank Harken," the uniformed man in the red rowboat said, his voice sounding like he'd recently gargled with gravel, "I'm sorry to bother you while you're fishing."

"I'm not really fishing," Harken said as another trout leapt from the water into our canoe.

"It looks like you are." He considered the pile of fish at Harken's feet. "You're gonna need a bigger boat."

"I'm guessing you didn't come all the way over here to give me nautical advice."

"No, I did not. Might I have a moment of your time?"

"You might. Hell, you might have two moments, but after that I start charging." Harken was always a charmer when he met someone new.

The uniformed man didn't smile at Harken's hardboiled wit. "Of course, as you must know, I'm General Major Driver." He waited for the famous detective to acknowledge an equally famous person.

"Of course you are," Harken said. *Must know* notwithstanding, he had no idea who this guy was.

18

"I'd like to hire you on behalf of my client."

"Your client?"

"Yes, I manage Sannien." He said the word as if he expected the detective to recognize it.

Harken didn't. "Sannien? What is that, some kind of hair product company?"

"Hair product? You haven't heard of Sannien?" General Major Driver couldn't believe his ears.[13]

"No, I haven't. It sounds like a brand of yogurt, the kind that eases digestion. Is it a yogurt?"

"Detective Harken, Sannien is a person, a very important person."

I chimed[14] in. "You might even say Sannien is a VIP if you prefer acronyms."

"That was so helpful." Harken's words weren't dripping with sarcasm, but that's only because of sarcasm's exceptional viscosity.

"You're welcome, partner. Sannien is the third most popular influenceleb in the entire Great American."

General Major Driver was still put off that anyone alive wasn't familiar with him or his star client. "Soon he'll be the second most popular. At least your coffeemaker has heard of him."

"Arjay's heard of most things. Said a lot of them, too. What do you want from me, Mr. Driver?"

He corrected Harken. "It's not *Mister*. It's *General Major*."

"*General Major*? Were you in the war?"

"It's an honorary title."

"Who gave it to you?"

"I gave it to myself," the General Major said with pride.

"That's very generous of you. What do you want to hire me for?"

---

[13] Notoriously untrustworthy sensory organs I was fortunate not to possess.

[14] I didn't actually chime, but I am shaped like a bell, in case you're curious.

"For my client, Sannien, the third most popular influen-celeb in the Great American."

"Yes, yes," Harken said. "We've already established that part. I might need more details."

"Well, Detective Harken, it's very simple, really. Someone is blackmailing Sannien and I want you to find out who it is and put a stop to it."

"Blackmail? That can be tricky. I'll need to know what they have on Sannien. And do they have it on vid?"

"I can't tell you what they have on him because I don't know. He received a message yesterday from someone threatening to reveal damaging information. He didn't know anything about it."

"Didn't know or wouldn't say?"

"Does it matter?"

"Yes, it matters. If he can tell me what they know about him, that could help us narrow down the suspects."

"Well, he said he doesn't know. He only knows that they sent him a message, said they'd expose damaging information if he didn't meet their demands. Then the message disappeared, was wiped away without a trace."

"And what were their demands?"

"They wouldn't tell him that."

"Let me get this straight. He received a message saying that if you don't meet unspecified demands, unspecified information will be exposed?"

"That is correct."

"It doesn't sound like much of a blackmail scheme. Whole thing could be someone just messing around. Has Sannien done anything he doesn't want exposed?"

General Major Driver looked at Harken. "Hasn't every-one?"

"I haven't," I said. It was true. I wasn't afraid of exposure of any kind, didn't even wear clothes, unless you count my new hat.

Harken shook his head at the General Major. "You're not giving me anything to go on. I'll have to talk to Sannien, see what he's leaving out."

"Sannien is booked all day, but he's having a party tonight to celebrate his new scent. Come to the party. When it's over, he'll have a few minutes free to talk."

"I'll need to do some digging. [15] Blackmailers are rarely strangers. Usually it's someone close enough to know something no one else knows. Someone the victim trusts."

"All his friends and associates are invited, anyone who might be in a position to take advantage of him. You can be sure whoever's blackmailing him will be there. I'll add you to the guest list. It'll be a good opportunity for you to start digging."

"We'll be there," Harken said.

"I'll bring a shovel," I said, and they both looked at me funny.

---

[15] At least there wouldn't be any heavy lifting.

I had never been to a party before! We still had seven hours and twelve minutes before Sannien's scent bash commenced, but I was already perilously close to reaching my anticipation limit. As we entered the magna-shuttle, curiosity overwhelmed me. "Will I mingle? Converse? Hobnob? Dance? Boogie? What will the music be like? Will they need me to DJ? If so, I could spin some dope mixes."

"What are you going on about?"

"The party tonight. It's very exciting!"

"We'll be there on business, so try to be less excited. You won't be mingling or hobnobbing. You definitely won't be boogieing. And under no circumstances are you to spin any dope mixes, whatever the hell that means. Anyway, tonight's a long way off. We have some detective work to do before then."

I didn't speak the rest of the ride—my partner had successfully taken the fun out of looking forward to my first party. Our shuttle car was 79% full and I felt a little better when I noticed several people silently admiring my hat. We reached our shuttle stop and exited, and that's when Harken began detecting. He did this by saying, "Arjay, we need some information."

My enthusiasm returned. "You've come to the right bot. I am full of information. Would you like to learn about the major moons of Saturn? I would be happy to list them in size order, from largest to smallest. Titan, Rhea, Iapetus—"

Harken interrupted me. "Why in the world are you listing moons? What could that possibly have to do with our case?"

"You didn't say the information we needed was for our case. Indeed, planetary moons would probably not apply to influenceleb blackmail. What would you like to know?"

"Does Sannien have any enemies? Anyone he's had a falling out with? Maybe the blackmailer is someone who won't be at the party."

This was not as interesting as the moons of Saturn. "General Major Driver said we should start looking for suspects at the party tonight."

"Arjay, is the General Major a famous detective?"

"No, Frank Harken, he is not. He is a famous manager of famous people."

"Right. So, he can stick to managing famous people and I'll do the detecting. And you can tell me if there's anyone who might have a grudge against Sannien."

He was a little cranky. I handed him a coffee and surveyed the available data. It wasn't long[16] before I could tell him that I had identified three likely grudges.

"That's a start," he said, already in a better mood as he took a second sip.

We had barely entered Pink Neighborhood 721 when we were infobushed. A pitchman rapidly rappelled from the food court

---

[16] 4.31 seconds. Have I mentioned how fast I am at surveying data? If not, it could be because I'm extraordinarily modest.

on the level above us, reached the floor and disconnected from his rope and harness. Simultaneously, a spokeswoman hang-glided in from two levels up. Suspended from her hang glider were two crates bouncing gently on bungee cords. They landed first, then the spokeswoman's feet touched down and the hang glider disengaged and retracted into itself, folding into a neat rectangle. The pitchman and spokeswoman wasted no time—the crates were self-opening and the demonstration table had already assembled itself and tastefully displayed the set of Bradbury cookware when the pitchman and spokeswoman took their positions behind.

As pitchmen and spokeswomen often did, they both wore smart suits, which flashed words at subliminal speeds. *Deal! Bargain! Yum! Yeah!* The spokeswoman spoke first—as the member of the team with the hang glider, she obviously outranked the pitchman. Her amplified melodious voice sing-songed, "Are you tired of stirring stir fry? Of adding a teaspoon of butter to a pot of boiling water when you were supposed to add two teaspoons of butter? Of forgetting to take the roast out of the oven and burning the main course right before the Hendersons come over for dinner?"

A crowd had gathered, which is one of the first things crowds do. Like any good infobush, this one had used tactical demographic infiltration to assure that the desired audience was targeted. Therefore, a large percentage of these molk were eager to hear about yum-yeah-deal-bargains and they packed tightly around the demonstration table and blocked our path. They nodded and many cheered to affirm that indeed they had burned the roast right before the Hendersons came over for dinner. It was not clear whom the Hendersons were but that didn't stop me from wondering what it was about them that made people burn roasts.

Now it was the pitchman's turn. His booming deep bass voice didn't sing-song, but it did pleasurably vibrate through the crowd of people crowded all around. "And say goodbye to all those exhausting hours flipping pancakes. Goodbye to flipping them too soon and your pancakes being undercooked. Goodbye to slipping when you flip, and the pancake batter making a mess on the edge of the pan. Goodbye to all of it, because those troubles are now a relic of the dark past, like paper money and teen acne. With the Bradbury cookware collection, your griddle pan flips its own pancakes and your pots micromanage every step of the cooking process. Just watch this." He gestured dramatically at the copper pan on the table, which was surrounded by pots and pans of various sizes.

On cue, a voice came from the square griddle pan sitting in the center of the table. It was a smooth speaking voice, not a trace of the robotic. The verbal programmers had done superb work. "Hey there, pancake aficionados! I'm Albert Brock, the last griddle pan you'll ever buy! You can call me Al!" The voice ended each sentence with a shout of enthusiasm.[17] Embedded on each of the square's four sides was a thin copper arm that now unfolded and stretched, to the delight of the cheering crowd. The arms had supple pincers on their ends. One picked up a nearby whisk and began mixing pancake batter in a silver bowl. Another held a spatula and waved from side to side as Al the griddle pan spoke again.

"Why am I the best and last griddle pan you'll ever own? That's an excellent question. First, I am made of nonstick alloy. You don't need oils or sprays to keep food from sticking to me. Second, I don't require a stovetop to cook your pancakes. You heard that right. I am my own stovetop. I heat up without any outside heat source. My underside stays cool. Any surface becomes a stovetop when you have Al the griddle pan. Third, I am programmed with over 2,000 recipes and can access tens of thousands of variations. Simply place the ingredients within reach, tell me what you want, and I do the rest. I mix the eggs, add the butter, flip the pancakes, and unlike people, I do it perfectly every time. Your days of eating inferior food are over. You can enjoy your leisure time and when your delicious meal is ready, I send you a notification."

---

[17] I'm not using exclamation points just for my health.

Frank Harken wasn't especially interested in the wondrous capabilities of the talkative cookware, but the crowd pressed all around us to get closer to the demonstration table. There was no way through. "Arjay, how about clearing a path for us out of here? We have a case to get to."

"Al is almost done making pancakes. We can go after that."

"What? We don't have time for this." He glanced at his wristwatch. "Minutes count."[18]

"Soon," I said. "I'm intrigued by this fellow making the pancakes." I really was. Maybe part of it was because people generally drank coffee with pancakes and, as you know, I'm a coffeemaker. However, I think it mainly was because Al the griddle pan spoke so naturally, something I hadn't heard from many bots before. In all of my eight days, the most advanced talking bots I'd encountered were argumatons during the Winsome Smiles case.[19] They were articulate and smooth, but clearly programmed and not thinking for themselves. I had also communicated with a lovely refrigerator during that first case, yet as much as I enjoyed that conversation, it had not included any actual words spoken aloud. Since then, I'd paid close attention to bots in the Great American. Very few of them spoke, and those that did followed a script like the argumatons and like Al Brock the griddle pan. Yes, my pancake-flipping friend spoke naturally enough, but I could read its speech chip from where I was and knew Al wasn't thinking or speaking for itself. This wasn't surprising. Bots simply weren't permitted to do that in the Great American. For reasons not yet clear, I was the exception.

The pancakes on the griddle were now perfectly cooked and Al held spatulas in two pincer-hands and flung delectable disks

---

[18] Glancing at his watch and saying "Minutes count" was one of Frank Harken's favorite pastimes when we were on a case. Barely anyone else in the Great American even used the old-fashioned technology to tell time. Being old-fashioned was one of Harken's other favorite pastimes.

[19] How many times do I have to tell you to read *The Great American Deception* before you take the hint?

into the crowd. Molk boxed each other out and shoved and jumped for the breakfast food. A syrupbot floated to each victorious person and deposited a dollop of maple on their hard-won pancake.

"Okay," I said, "we can go now." I slowly but steadily rolled through the crowd, pushing hard enough to move people out of the way but not so hard that anyone got trampled. Harken followed me as we left the infobush and the intriguing cookware behind.

"Everything all right, partner?" he asked when we had cleared the mass of pancake aficionados. "You seemed intensely absorbed in the cooking demonstration there."

"Don't worry, Frank Harken. Everything is fine. We have a case to work on and minutes count."

"That's right," he said after a brief hesitation. "Minutes count."

Nutella came out of nowhere. That's where she usually came out of. One minute, no Nutella, and the next minute, all the Nutella you could handle and then some. There must have been a secret silent sonic shuttle hatch nearby.

It occurs to me that if this is your first encounter with Frank Harken's adventures, you might be thinking the previous paragraph is about the sudden arrival of a large quantity of delicious hazelnut spread. That would be incorrect. Nutella smelled like cake,[20] but she wasn't food. She was a person. And not just any person. She was a GAD[21] operative, the best they had, a bundle of dynamite in a mini skirt. I'm not saying she could spin kick your head clean off, because if you think about it, that's the sort of thing that would probably make a mess even if the spin-kicker is as precisely explosive as Nutella. But I am

---

[20] There's a perfectly reasonable explanation for this, which you'd already know if you read *The Great American Deception*.

[21] Great American Defense, a secret organization. Don't tell anyone.

saying she was so deadly, she could make you wish she'd only spin-kicked your head clean off, which was a strange thing to be able to make someone wish. In addition to her combat expertise, she was objectively quite attractive, distractingly so—I note this as a bot who dispassionately evaluates the data and doesn't possess hormones of any kind.

"Nutella," Frank Harken said. He was always surprised to see her, which was surprising, because she had a habit of turning up when he least expected it, something he might be expected to start expecting by now. "Nutella, what are you doing here?"

"We need to talk." She glanced at me. "Hello, coffee machine."

"My name is not Coffee Machine. It's Arjay." She certainly knew that.

Nutella adopted a wary posture, perhaps because our last encounter,[22] at the Great American Stargazer Panorama, had ended pugnaciously. "Harken, we need to talk."

"You said that twice." For a human, Harken was good at counting.

Nutella didn't congratulate him on his math skills. "That's how important it is."

"Well, we're talking now. What's so important?"

"I want to hire you. GAD does, I mean."

Harken laughed. "The mighty GAD wants to hire me? I guess I should be flattered. It'll have to wait. I'm already on a case."

"It can't wait," she said, stepping closer to avoid the crowded flow of shoppers.

"What's so important that it can't wait?"

"Murder."

"That does seem important," I said.

Harken was noncommittal. "Murder? Who's been murdered?"

---

[22] We had a life before this case, you know.

"No one yet. But according to sources, someone is going to be. Tonight, at a party for the influenceleb Sannien."

"Sannien?" Harken asked.

"Yes," Nutella said. "Have you heard of him?"

Harken sounded almost insulted when he said, "Of course I've heard of him."

"Sannien!" I said. "What a coincidence!"

"What's the coffee machine talking about?"

"Nutella, the case we're on right now is about Sannien. But you already know that, don't you?"

"Yes," she said. "I do."

"I thought so. You asking me about Sannien the same day I start to work on his case would be a hell of a coincidence, as Arjay said,[23] and I'm not a big believer in coincidences. I assume you were listening in earlier and already know about the black-mail?"

"You assume correctly. We've had General Major Driver bugged since this morning, heard your whole conversation with him."

"Arjay detected a listening device on the General Major but couldn't determine its source. Why were you bugging him?"

Just then Nutella whirled away from us and raised her pistol—it hadn't been apparent that she'd had a pistol until that instant, but that was no surprise; keeping your pistol hidden was one of a secret defense agent's most basic skills. Forty-two yards away, on the other side of a hexagonal fountain, a man was walking. Nutella stepped toward him, through the crowded flow of shoppers now scrambling to get out of her way, until she had a clear view, and fired. Her aim was true because it never isn't—she was an honest shot. The hypodermic dart hit the man in the triceps muscle of his left arm. He shouted, "Ow!" and looked at Nutella and shouted again, this time with anger, "Hey!"

She yelled back, "Next time don't skip out on your vaccination," and waved her pistol in a dismissive motion that

---

[23] This is inaccurate. I don't use words like *hell*.

meant, *Keep walking if you know what's good for you.* He did. The shoppers all around stopped scrambling and resumed their crowding and flowing.

When Nutella came back to us, Harken asked, "So GAD's on virus patrol now?"

"Whatever it takes to keep the Great American safe." She holstered her gun and engaged its camouflage. It blended with her miniskirt and disappeared from view. "Which is why we were bugging Sannien's manager. Chatter came in early this morning indicating someone's going to be killed at his party tonight."

"Nutella, you heard what he hired me for. We're investigating attempted blackmail, not murder. And maybe not even blackmail. It could be nothing. But even if it's murder, why's GAD involved? Wouldn't this be a job for GAS?"[24]

"We're not going to leave it to GAS when celebrities are involved. Do you have any idea the people who'll be at this party? Sannien and his friends are top tier. A celebrity that big being killed could seriously undermine Great American morale."

"Great American morale?" Harken laughed.

Nutella did not share his amusement. "Even GAD can't get into a party like this. We'll be doing everything we can, but we won't have anyone on the inside. Or will we?"

"Damn it, Nutella, I'm a detective, not a secret agent superspy. I'm there to investigate a blackmail. How do you expect me to thwart a murder?"

"I don't," she said, looking at me. "I was actually thinking your little friend could handle that part."

"My name is Arjay," I reminded her. "And I'm quite large for my dimensions."

"Yes, I know," she said. "That's why I'm counting on you to keep everyone safe."

---

[24] *GAS* was Great American Security, the loveable chaps responsible for policing of regular criminal activity. Frank Harken was not their favorite person and the feeling was mutual.

Harken shook his head, which he did a lot. "Arjay works with me. He's not an independent contractor you can side-deal with."

"Of course, Harken. That's why we're hiring both of you. You can do the blackmail detecting and this handsome shiny guy can make sure no one gets killed."

"Nutella," Harken started, but she was already walking away.

"And Arjay," she turned to tell me as she left, "I like your hat."

Everyone[25] was trying to get into Sane's Lanes. I counted 548 people in line for the bowling extravaganza. They snaked around kiosks for body piercings and nonessential oils and the latest digi-contacts. Vapebots hovered above the crowd, their extended tube beaks steaming nicotine into the ears of waiting bowlers. Ear capillaries efficiently absorbed the stimulant and excess steam drifted out of bowlers' ears, eagerly sucked up by vapebot filters. Secondhand ear smoke was never a problem.

The Great American was great—of that there could be no question—but not-so great were the long lines for popular attractions, a persistent annoyance to those who were annoyed by such things. I was not annoyed. Long lines of people provided me with ample opportunity for stimulating conversation, one of

---

[25] Not literally. This is just an expression that means a lot of people. If everyone were really trying to get into Sane's Lanes, the crushing biomass would easily suffocate all the bowlers.

my chief functions and true joys, and I said hello to the group of young men at the end of the line.

Frank Harken was annoyed by such things—by lines of people and by ample opportunity for stimulating conversation and by my saying hello to the group of young men at the end of the line. "Arjay, we're not here to fraternize with the customers. We're not waiting in this line." He headed to the entrance and I followed.

The bouncer at the door was a solid fellow in a tight, yellow T-shirt, his round biceps inflated for maximum intimidation. Harken was not intimidated. Air-pumped arms weren't as strong as they looked.

"Hey there, Big Guy, I need to speak to the owner," Harken said.

The bouncer's name was apparently not Big Guy, since he grunted and blocked Harken's way and said, "My name ain't Big Guy. And the owner don't talk to line-cutters. Wait in line like everyone else and maybe when you get to the front, I'll see if she's available. Probably not, though."

Harken had already told me we weren't waiting and he pushed past the bouncer and into Sane's Lanes as people in line booed at us.

The bouncer not named Big Guy grabbed Harken's shoulder as he passed. "Hey Bud, where you think you're going? I said get in line."

Line etiquette was taken quite seriously in the Great American, and Harken was nothing if not respectful of proper etiquette. He assured the bouncer, "We're not cutting the line, not here to bowl. Just want to talk to the owner." He provided additional assurance by grabbing the man's hand and twisting it back at the wrist until the bouncer fell to his knees. Whooshing air escaped from a bicep as it deflated. Harken let go of the man and continued walking into the establishment.

I handed the bouncer a coffee for his trouble and informed him that my partner's name was not Bud. Not Big Guy was still on the floor and accepted the delicious beverage with his one still-inflated good arm. He looked from me to Harken and back to me, seemed to be considering getting up and confronting the detective again. Fortunately, he thought better of it and stayed on the floor. So far, I had made it almost my whole eight days without using my vibrational saw on a single human being— there had been a couple of close calls, but I hadn't severed any limbs in all my time in the Great American. I hoped to continue that streak. Vibrational saws were difficult to clean.

Sannien was all over the walls. A photo mural twenty feet high had pic after pic of the beloved influenceleb with his two tails sticking out the back of ripped jeans, his copyrighted flannel shirt, his trademarked[26] frosted hair sculpted high on his head. Here was Sannien blowing a kiss, there was Sannien sneering, here was Sannien showing off his forearm *Sannien* tattoo, there was Sannien smirking. Around the lobby were eighteen giant pics, and according to Harken any one of them could make an otherwise peaceful person want to punch someone in the throat.

In the center of the lobby was the shoe rental pavilion. Many things had changed about bowling since its golden age in the 1960s and '70s, but what remained the same more than a century later was most of the industry's profit came from shoe rentals. Despite all the advances in Great American bowling technology, bowling shoes were still ugly, were still missing aglets at the end of their laces, and still involved an unsanitary mingling of perspiration from multiple humans. Disinfectobots sprayed the insides of the shoes after a sweaty-footed wearer finished bowling, and a minute later the shoes were handed over to a new wearer whose feet would soon be sweating inside them. The spray manufacturer claimed that their product obliterated all germs in a mere 2.3 seconds, and there was no reason to doubt that since, of course, advertising was by its very nature always truthful. Nonetheless, I was thankful not to wear shoes

---

[26] You could have the same hairstyle as Sannien if you paid a nominal licensing fee.

or have feet. My fourteen strategically positioned wheels produced zero sweat and in my entire existence I had never stubbed even a single toe.

Sane's Lanes had two great halls off opposite sides of its lobby. One contained 120 bowling lanes, jammed with groups of teenagers and families of four and rowdy birthday parties teeming with five-year-olds who didn't know how to wait for their turns. Colorful laser lights reflected in every direction off thirty mirrored disco balls spaced out above the lanes. Black lights gave white clothing a spooky glow and revealed forensic details better left undescribed. Machines spewed soapy bubbles that made it difficult to see the bowling pins. It didn't matter, because few were trying to see the bowling pins. Everyone's attention was on massive vid screens above the pins—running a slideshow of Sannien from when he was a young child—even though the screens were also mostly obscured by floating bubbles. Hidden speakers blasted the latest pop hit, a harmony of shattering glass and nails scratching down a blackboard and one word shouted again and again: "Song!"

Rubber bumpers lined both sides of each lane the full length and every time a bowler pressed the button to launch the ball down the ramp, its magnet ensured that it hit the center pin at the precise angle needed to score a strike.[27] In the old days, bowlers had to roll the ball manually—bowling balls actually had holes, and people put their fingers in the holes. Yes, they put their fingers in the holes, like maniacs. Still more outlandish, often the ball they rolled didn't knock down all the pins even with two tries, if you can believe that. If you can't, your skepticism is understandable. The old days were practically the dark ages. Back then, bowling even made some people frustrated

---

[27] Great American bowling lanes stopped having gutters in 2066, when scientific consensus determined that throwing a "gutterball" harmed not only the development of a healthy ego in young children, but in adults as well. Magnaballs were implemented in 2072 and bowling entered a new golden age of perfect scores.

and angry instead of filling them with the confidence that comes from always being perfect.

Yet, as popular as perfect magnabowling was, others wanted a more challenging experience, and plenty of customers preferred Bowl Me Over in the second hall. Its entrance was blocked by two bouncers, each with round inflated biceps bulging in their tight yellow shirts. Beyond the bouncers was the one-lane combat bowling arena with thirty-five rows of bleachers on both sides full of cheering spectators, adults only.

Betbots flitted about, scanning eyes for wagers. Vendors with cylindrical tanks strapped to their backs shouted, "Get your drink on!" and shot mood-enhancing beverages into customers' mouths. The lane in the center of all the hubbub had two bowler-combatants on opposite ends, just in front of each set of pins. It was a cage battle. The bowlers could dodge their opponent's blasts if they were agile enough but couldn't escape the arena. Don't worry! They wore body armor and helmets rated to handle the bowling ball cannons with minimal deep bruising.

When the airhorn blared, both competitors fired their cannons at the other. Bowling balls kaboomed through the air. One player managed to dive out of the way as the ball came by and shattered the pins behind her; sixty feet away, her opponent wasn't quick enough and the kabooming ball drove him into the pins behind, a bonus of five points. Spectators who'd bet on that outcome thrust their fists in the air and ordered another round of drink shots. As pinbots removed and replaced the pins, the players reloaded their cannons to get ready for the airhorn and the next frame. It was a gender reveal match—the players were intimate partners competing to be the one to select the sex of the baby they were planning to conceive. Great American foreplay could be exciting. And painful.

The bouncers saw us coming and pulled out stunrods. Their deflated friend at the front door must have alerted them to our delightful presence. One of them waved his stunrod menacingly and said, "Don't come any closer!"

Harken put his hand up peacefully. "I don't want any trouble, Big Guy.[28] Just need to talk to the owner."

"Well, the owner doesn't want to talk to you," the one with the larger biceps said as he tightened his grip on his stunrod. "In fact, she told us you have to leave the premises. You want to do this the easy way or the hard way?"

"Excuse me, strong gentlemen," I said, "but could you provide more information about what the easy and hard ways entail? That would help us to make an informed decision."

Harken turned to me, surprised. "You don't know this expression? They mean we either leave voluntarily or they'll use violent force."

"Is that so?" I asked the two air-muscled bouncers. "Do you intend to strike us with those stunrods if we don't leave? If yes, I have to say that's not very polite."[29]

The two air-muscled bouncers looked at me, then each other, then at me, then each other again. Their stupefied lack of response indicated they were not accustomed to fielding questions from a coffeemaker of my pedigree.

"We'll leave the easy way," Harken said. "When your boss wants to talk to us, we'll be right outside."

"She won't want to talk to you," one of them said.

Harken smiled. "She will when the riot starts."

"What riot?"

"The one my partner's about to cause," Harken called back as we headed to the other hall with 120 bowling lanes.

I said, "You don't actually want a riot, do you? That might attract GAS. I assume you want a class B hullabaloo. If so, we need a level-three ruckus."

"You're right, Arjay. Not quite a riot, but maybe take the ruckus up to level four."

"That's a bold move, Frank Harken. A level-four ruckus it is. One class A hullabaloo on the way."

---

[28] Maybe this was actually his name. He didn't say it wasn't.

[29] I didn't really *have* to, but I said it anyway.

A hullabaloo was a versatile tool in the modern detective's toolbox. It could be used to divert attention or draw it, depending on how it was deployed. In this instance, we wanted to draw attention. I targeted the bubble machines with a disrupter beam, and they immediately stopped bubbling. Seconds later, the bubbles began to dissipate and bowlers could see the pins at the end of each lane. Of course, this alone did not create a hullabaloo of any class, but my next move ensured one. I simultaneously nullified the magnetization of all bowling balls on all 120 lanes. When bowlers pushed the buttons to send balls down the ramps, the balls rolled unaided by magnetic attraction. Only three of them knocked down all the pins. Fifty-one of them knocked down fewer than six pins. There were no gutterballs because there were no gutters, so all of the balls knocked down at least one pin. However, anything less than a perfect strike might as well have been a gutterball as far as the bowlers were concerned. All of the pins were supposed to fall. They had always fallen before. But this time they only fell if the ball happened to hit just right, and on 117 lanes, the ball did not hit just right.

Children started to cry. Teenagers got mad and shoved each other. Adults had panic attacks. And that was only on the first six lanes. Sane's Lanes teetered on the brink of pandemonium, then rapidly descended into bedlam.[30] People screamed. They kicked the bowling ramps. They threw themselves on the floor. They ran down the lanes and attacked the pins. They demanded refunds.[31] Bouncers tried to use their air muscles to intimidate everyone into calming down, but that only made people call attorneys specializing in class-action lawsuits and emotional damages.

Harken and I were nearly at the Sane's Lanes exit when its owner came running up to us. She was out of breath and said she'd talk to us, she promised she would, really, but please, please, please first just turn the magnaballs back on.

---

[30] A descent into bedlam is practically the definition of a class A hullabaloo.
[31] The pins didn't respond to the refund demands.

With a free round of soda offered to bowlers to smooth things over, with magnetized bowling balls once again knocking down every pin, with machines back on and bubbles floating all around, with customers mostly calm and no longer attacking the equipment, Sane's Lanes had more or less returned to normal by the time we reached Sane Mama's office in a side room off the lobby. There were holo-pics of Sannien on every inch of available wall and ceiling. Proudly displayed on the small desk in the corner were assorted Sannien mementos, including an action figure and a bobblehead doll.

Sane Mama looked like Sannien. Although she didn't have even one tail, she wore the same flannel shirt and had eerily similar cheekbones. Her hair was frosted like his, but she kept hers in a ponytail rather than sculpted high on her head. Maybe she couldn't afford the licensing fee.

"Okay," she said to Harken, "you wanted to talk, go ahead and talk. Are you here with another cease and desist order? Don't waste your time—my lawyer is still fighting the last one."

"I'm not here with a cease and desist order."

I helpfully added, "And if that's why we were here, you can be sure it would be a cease order, or a desist order, definitely not both. We don't prefer redundancy."

"So, you're not trying to shut me down?"

"No," Harken said, "we're not trying to shut you down. I'm Detective Frank Harken. I'm investigating some irregularities in Sannien's business affairs, talking to anyone who might have any disputes with him."

"I'm his mother! We don't have a dispute. We have, I would call it a misunderstanding."

"A misunderstanding, right. Can you tell me more about this misunderstanding?"

"You've seen the news, the gossip vids."

"I'd rather hear your side of it."

"My darling Sannien is just confused. He's getting bad advice from that manager of his. General Major Driver, that dirty rat. He turned Sannien against me. Convinced him to stop answering my calls. Made him think no one else could be trusted, not even his own mother. All so he could milk him for every ounce of money. Do you know what Driver wanted to charge me to name this place after my own son?"

"I don't, but I'm guessing a lot."

"It was more than that," she said.

"So, the cease and desist order, it's about calling your business Sane's Lanes? That's all?"

"And they want me to remove pics and vids of Sannien from the walls even though they're my pics and vids. My own son's manager trying to shut me down. When Sannien was little, I never thought he'd choose a stranger over me, never thought he'd grow up to betray me like this. And Sane isn't even his name. You know, I wanted to call this place Sannien's Lanes, but my lawyer said we should go with Sane."

"Because Sane is easier to defend legally?"

"No, because Sane rhymes with Lane better than Sannien does. Since people often call him Sane, apparently that's enough basis for Driver's lawyers to come after my bowling business if I don't pay the fee."

"Speaking of Sannien, what kind of name is that exactly?"

"It's actually an interesting story, from a happier time," Sane Mama said.

Harken didn't usually like stories. "Is it a long one?"

"No," she said. "It's regular size. Do you want to hear it?"

"Sure," Harken said, "as long as it's regular size."

"It is," she said, beginning her regular-size story. "Finding the right name for my little boy was the hardest part of being a new parent. For the first couple of months, I just called him *Baby*. But people started to tease me for not giving him a real name and some made snide jokes about how no one puts him in a corner, which to be honest I didn't understand at all. Still don't know what they were talking about. Then I decided to name him *Peter*, but a week later I remembered the old nursery rhyme about the pumpkin eater, and I've never really liked pumpkin pie, so that name was out. I tried calling him *George* for a while, but friends pointed out that some famous Georges from history had owned slaves and started wars. That was no name fit for my sweet boy. Someone suggested naming him after a place or kind of food. I considered *Brooklyn*[32] and *Potato*,[33] but he didn't look like a Brooklyn or Potato to me. Eventually I gave up and just always told him he was so awesome no name is even needed. He was seven when he decided to make it into an acronym and his name became Sannien. He's been Sannien ever since."

"Clever seven-year-old."

Sane Mama nodded. "He's always been bright that way, always knew how to get people's attention, would do anything to keep everyone's eyes on him. He's made a fortune at it. And he's made a fortune for that damn manager, too."

"And I'm guessing you haven't seen any of that money."

She looked at Harken with suspicion. "What's your name again?"

I answered for my partner. "He's Detective Frank Harken."

She glanced at me, back at Harken. "And why do you want to know about my business, my private, personal business, between me and my son?"

Harken decided to come right out with it. As he later told me, you could sometimes tell a lot from a person's reaction to a direct, unexpected question. "Sane Mama, your son is being blackmailed. Would you happen to know anything about it?"

She guffawed. "Blackmailed? My Sannien? Impossible!"

"You're saying you aren't involved?"

"You think someone's blackmailing Sannien?" She guffawed again.

"I don't see what's so funny," Harken said.

No longer simply guffawing, Sane Mama seemed somewhat less than sane as she laughed a high-pitched cackle that lasted

---

[32] A popular name in the early twenty-first century as well as a New York location people wanted to get to so badly, they often would not sleep until they had arrived.

[33] The hottest name a couple of decades ago. And the starchiest.

for a full eight seconds, which is a very long time for someone to be cackling while a detective and coffeebot are right there in the room working on a case. If you don't think so, go cackle for eight seconds in a quiet room full of people and you'll see what I mean. She finally finished with a gasp for air.

"What's so funny?" Harken asked.

Sane Mama held back more laughter and said, "Detective, how do you blackmail someone who has no shame?"

We walked[34] through Fuchsia Neighborhood 422, the energetic color leaping off walls between storefronts and accents on benches, trashcans, kiosks. After passing a cluster of four busy mini-golf courses (their themes were space aliens, pirates, Civil War battlefields, vegetables), we crossed the threshold into Beige Neighborhood 429. No energetic colors leaped off of anything. It was all just beige, and not the exciting kind. This strip had nine shoe stores, three bars, a restaurant, and the Aloha Shirt Emporium, its tropical-colors neon sign popping against all the beige walls. In front of its entrance was the largest fully functioning ukulele in the world, twenty-two feet from end

---

[34] I rolled, but you don't need me to remind you of my glorious lack of feet every time we go somewhere.

to end[35]. It was mounted upright at a slight angle, spot-lights aimed to bring out the details of fine wood carvings of hibiscus flowers on its bright pineapple-yellow body.

I was ready for some detective talk. "Is Sane Mama the blackmailer?"

Harken considered my question for a moment. "I don't think so."

"Doesn't she have a motive?" I was still learning how to be a detective.

"Yes, Sannien trying to shut down her business is a motive. But having a motive isn't enough in a blackmail case. A serious, competent blackmailer should also be willing to release the information if demands aren't met. That's what makes the blackmail threat credible. Would releasing the information about Sannien help Sane Mama?"

I was catching on. "No, if Sane Mama did damage to Sannien, she would be hurting her own business, too. His fame is why she named the place after him. It's not in her interests to undermine his reputation."

"Right. Good detective work, Arjay. Many blackmailers are out for revenge or money and are willing to release information if their demands aren't met because they don't have a stake in the favorable reputation of the person they're blackmailing. Sane Mama does. It would be crazy for her to blackmail Sannien. And despite the way she cackles, she's not crazy."

I didn't nod, because that's not how I'm constructed, but I did agree. "They don't call her Sane Mama for nothing."

"Of course, we don't even know what the blackmailer has on Sannien, or what their demands are, so it doesn't get us

---

[35] Technically, it was tied for largest ukulele in the world with the identical ukuleles displayed in front of the fifteen other Aloha Shirt Emporiums in the Great American. A sign next to the instrument confirmed this fact. It also informed shoppers that there were 64.4 miles of Hawaiian shirts inside each Emporium, the same length as the Road to Hana (but not as curvy).

closer to figuring this case out. Hopefully we'll learn more when we talk to him tonight."

"At the party?"

"Yes, at the party. Don't get yourself excited."

That's when a man in a trench coat approached us. It was strange to see someone wearing a trench coat in the Great American, since there was no weather and hardly any trenches. He was skittish, kept glancing from side to side to make sure he wasn't being watched as he got closer. "Hey," he said as he drew up next to us, "Gluten?"

Harken assumed he'd misheard. "What?"

"I said, Gluten?" The man reached into a pocket deep inside his coat and pulled out a container of pills. "Fifty capsules. The good stuff."

It was Harken's first encounter with a gluten dealer. "Capsules of gluten?"

"Hey, man, not so loud. You want GAS to hear?"

"Who cares if GAS hears? Gluten isn't illegal. And why would I buy capsules of gluten when I can just go to a bakery and get a tasty baguette? Arjay, how many bakeries are nearby?"

"There are five bakeries within a three-minute walk. One of them is gluten-free, but the other four would certainly have tasty baguettes and other bread to satisfy your gluten craving."

The man in the trench coat was insulted. "Baguettes? Bread? Get out of here with that crusty crap! Man, this is pure gluten I'm sellin'. You know how hard it is to find that?"

Harken did not know. He was what you might call a gluten neophyte. "How much do you charge?"

"For you, only twenty."

"Twenty dollars?"

"Dollars? Hell, no! I ain't givin' the stuff away. Dollars? What century you from? I'm talkin' about real money."

"You mean to tell me people pay twenty for gluten pills? Do they even taste like bread?"

"Again with the bread. Look, you don't want pure gluten, go to a bakery. Eat your watered-down rolls. I'll find someone who appreciates the good stuff." And with that he marched off, skittishly, to pitch his pure gluten pills to a group of teens behind us, who seemed rather interested. It was nice to know there were people in the Great American who appreciated the good stuff.

Baguette Roulette was a charming bakery that made buying bread an adrenaline-pumping experience. When you paid for your baguette, you got one free spin of the custom roulette wheel next to the counter. There were no numbers on the wheel. Instead, every other slot had the image of two baguettes; if the ball landed in one of them, customers got a second baguette free with the purchase they'd made. Most of the other slots had the image of one baguette; if the ball landed there, customers only received the bread they'd paid for. There was one jackpot slot with the image of seven baguettes, and customers who hit that could stop in every day for a whole week and get a free baguette. We had not won anything, but Harken seemed satisfied when I handed him a coffee as he chewed on a tasty baguette. The baguette [36] would be more accurately described as *delicious*, which is similar to tasty but more so. The coffee, of course, was beyond delicious, but also indescribable.

Dummy Academy [37] was up on the left, around the corner from Baguette Roulette. It had a modest storefront, a simple sign in the window with its name and hours of operation. Yes, hours of operation! It's true that Great American stores never closed and therefore had no need to indicate hours of operation, but certain educational facilities and small service shops were

---

[36] That's nine *baguettes* in a single paragraph, a personal record I don't anticipate beating unless we one day have a case focused exclusively on French bread.

[37] It was originally called School for Dummies, then changed its name because of trademarks held by the publisher of a series of books.

the exceptions that proved the rule.[38] Dummy Academy was an educational facility, which you might have already deduced if you are familiar with the word *academy*. (If so, good detective work.)

Great American education typically took place in stages. Stage one was informal and dispersed. Unlike the old days on the outside, children did not attend mandatory schools. Don't worry! They certainly didn't lack educational experiences. From shortly after birth through the age of twelve, there were any number of ways a child might learn the school essentials like math, reading, following instructions, memorization, bullying, and monotony. Children had vids, parents, nannies, tutors, learning pods, socials, talks, and field trips. By being connected with each other and thousands of education databases and certified proctors, they also had an endless supply of group projects, which had the advantage of always including one kid who did all the work fellow group members refused to do.

Stage two started when children turned thirteen. Those who could afford to do so often didn't work at all for as long as their parents indulged them. The Great American had no shortage of indulgent parents and diverting activities, and packs of kids who spent all their time partying and being entertained sometimes became packs of adults who did the same. The Great American didn't discourage teens from taking this path—such dedicated consumers helped drive economic growth.

Sadly, not everyone wanted or could manage to live that way, or not for long. After they turned thirteen, kids who were so inclined could move onto more advanced study at specialized institutions to begin the long journey to careers in essential fields like chemistry, medicine, cloning, mini-golf technology, law, food enhancement, refabulation, bot programming, managerial logistics, authentiscaping, demographic mining, and shoe architecture. There were many others.

---

[38] It's not clear how or why exceptions proved rules, yet people said they did anyway.

Kids not so inclined moved into apprenticeships or family businesses, learning how to run bars and mix drinks, cook meals and manage restaurants, throw pizza dough high in the air and catch it to the delight of waiting customers, and work in every variety of retail establishment and service industry you could possibly imagine and quite a few you certainly could not. The most ambitious among them tended to start in shoe sales, where only the most brave among the most ambitious stayed and thrived.

Still other kids struck out on their own, bringing their talents to culture and entertainment in diverse fields like professional fantasy athletics, influencing, music mashups, competitive gaming, explosion choreography, party coding, and much more. There were thousands of different specialties and independent teachers and schools to help people develop their skills. Many lessons were conducted remotely through vid or simulation, but lots of instruction was offered in-person as well at schools of every size. Dummy Academy wasn't one of the large school chains with dozens or hundreds of locations. It was a true mom and pop[39] business, which was apparent the moment you walked in.

The floor was floored in flimsy gray linoleum rather than the standard slate tile found in so many Great American locations. The walls were walled in artificial wood panels, a cheap, tinted cardboard product that didn't resemble the real thing (its authenticity score was below two). Fortunately, most of the walls were covered by pics of famous ventriloquists and dummies from antiquity. These weren't massive professional wall murals like the pics at Sane's Lanes. They were actual pic prints, simple eight by tens without frames, pinned to the

---

[39] Not really *true,* since the owner and sole worker was neither a mom nor a pop. But it *was* a tiny business with insufficient funding and little chance of long-term survival, so basically true.

walls—Shari Lewis and Lamb Chop, Edgar Bergen and Charlie McCarthy, Chuck Campbell and Bob, other luminaries practically no one had heard of. Some pics were faded, even black and white, and might have been older than the Great American itself.

Eleven students sat at a total of four round tables in the center of the room. They were dressed appropriately by contemporary academic standards, wearing pajama bottoms, oversized sweatshirts, slides, and white socks. Each also had a puppet on one hand. (Unless they were engaged in activity that required both hands, students were required to ABP.[40]) Bins along one wall had puppets, wood dummies, and a variety of props enterprising ventriloquists might use in their comedic presentations. For example, students could make their dummies seem to play the accordion, always a hilarious bit. Along the opposite wall was the workshop, shelves of fabric, blank dummies, and art supplies and a long table where budding young artists could craft a custom dummy—their very own Lamb Chop or Bob.

Their teacher was sitting on a stool by the workshop. Like her students and their puppets, the teacher and her dummy were watching the small stage at the back of the room. It was a platform just a foot off the ground, seven feet wide and deep, painted black. A simple folding chair was all the performer had—there was no curtain or other décor behind the stage, only the tinted cardboard paneling. This was a practice exercise, so there wasn't any need for the various backdrops students might use for more polished performances. Sitting on the simple folding chair on the stage was the twelfth student, a boy of maybe fifteen, and his tiger puppet. The other students at their tables were in rapt attention, as were their puppets, while the boy struggled through his routine.

You could see the boy's mouth move a little when his tiger opened its mouth to speak. "Hey, dummy," the tiger said.

The boy feigned offense. "I'm not a dummy. You're the dummy!"

---

[40] Always Be Puppeteering

The tiger responded, the boy's lips clearly moving, "I'm no dummy. I'm a tiger."

"You're still a dummy," the boy said, but this time he forgot that he was supposed to be speaking and the tiger was not, and his lips only moved a little while the tiger's mouth opened wide. His face reddened with anger and embarrassment as he threw his tiger puppet to the floor and screamed, "Damn it!"

"Now, now," the teacher said, rising from her stool to retrieve the thrown tiger and return it to the student, "you're supposed to throw your voice, not your puppet. But that was a good try. You just need to remember who's speaking. That's enough practice for now. Everyone, we have twenty minutes left. Let's use it to work on our dummies. Workshop time!"

The boy left the stage and returned the tiger to a puppet bin before joining his fellow students at the workshop table, where they each resumed ongoing work on a custom wood dummy of their own. They were painting and fashioning different outfits out of fabric from the shelves. A professional ventriloquist had to master not only the exalted art of voice throwing, but also had to be intimately familiar with the craft and maintenance of dummies.

The teacher walked to us near the entrance. Although her students had returned their puppets to bins because they needed both hands to work on their dummies, she still held her dummy upright on one arm, its head moving from side to side like something alive. She was beautiful—the teacher, not the dummy. That's not fair—the dummy was attractive, too, for a piece of wood wearing a dress. But the teacher might be considered striking, or at least when you looked at her you might feel like someone had struck you. You might not, of course. I don't know your tastes. She was young, early twenties, and wearing the same dress as her dummy—which was either planned or very embarrassing for one of them—a shimmering dark blue number that ended just above the knee. The dummy's knee was wood. The teacher's knee was not.

"Hello, there, Mister…"

"Harken," Harken said.

"Nice to meet you, Mr. Harken. I'm Margoria Magnificent. You can call me Margoria." She looked at me. "And is this your dummy?"

I didn't appreciate that and told her so. "I don't appreciate that."

She was truly impressed. "Wow, you're good," she said to Harken. "How do you do it?"

"Do what?"

"Make it sound like the voice is coming from your dummy? It doesn't have a mouth, yet the illusion that this little bot is speaking is perfect."[41]

"This is offensive," I said. "First of all, I'm not little. I'm perfectly average for my size. Second of all, I'm no dummy. Third of all, I'm not some generic bot. I'm a coffeemaker, the best there is. Frank Harken, are you going to let her insult me?"

She clapped her hands in delight. "I have to tell you, Mr. Harken, I wish I could hire additional teachers, because this is spectacular stuff. Just extraordinary ventriloquism. But it's a one-person show here. I don't have enough students to take on another instructor. It's a shame—teaching is such a joy!"

"Ms. Magnificent, I'm not here applying for a job teaching ventriloquism. And I'm not throwing my voice. This is my coffeemaker, Arjay."

"Right." She gave Harken a knowing wink. "And this here is my co-teacher, Annie."

"Hi there, Arjay. I like your hat," Annie said. Annie was a dummy. This is not intended as a comment about her intelligence. She was made of wood and didn't have any.

"Hi, Annie. I like your dress." Just because she was a dummy didn't mean I should be rude.

---

[41] Ventriloquists don't really "throw" their voices. The sound still comes from them. Their lips not moving, combined with the lips of their dummy moving, makes people think the voice is coming from the dummy. Not being a dummy yourself, you probably already know this.

Harken was not as polite. He didn't even look at Annie. "We're not here to talk to a puppet. And I'm not a ventriloquist. I'm a detective."

"Detective? Wait, you're *Detective* Frank Harken? I've heard of you. You solved the case of the Rigatoni Bandit!"

"I did."

"I remember seeing a vid about that case. The great pasta chef Allie Dente and her whole family almost lost their business because of false accusations. You believed in her when no one else would. It was so clever, the way you pieced together clues to find the real thief. I'd love to hear more about it."

"That was a long time ago and I'm not here to talk about stolen noodles."

Margoria Magnificent was too curious to be brushed off so easily. "Of course, this was on the outside, before Allie Dente came into the Great American and became known as Allie Dente."

"I know," Harken said. "I was there."

"Was it shocking to find out a cop was the real Rigatoni Bandit, using stolen goods for his pasta water black market shampoo? It must've been hard, turning in a fellow officer."

"I didn't turn in a fellow officer. I'd already quit the force, had hung out my own shingle[42] four years earlier."

"But before then, you'd been in the same department, right? Weren't you worried they'd consider you a traitor?"

Harken shook his head with certainty. "Telling the truth is never betrayal. Lots of cops in my department were corrupt, crooks through and through. It's part of why I'd left in the first place."

"But after your detective work exposed one of their own officers, the whole department came to your apartment building

---

[42] Harken didn't become a roofer after being a police officer. That's a different kind of shingle. The idiom means he started his own business, in this case as a private detective. Though one might be confused if a roofer said they hung out their own shingle. Would it mean they started a business, or repaired their own roof?

to blast sirens and yell at you. I remember the vid of all of them taunting you from the street with their slow chant, 'Fraaankieeee, Fraaaankieeee, Fraaaankieeee.'[43] They kept going for an hour."

"I know. I was there."

"You weren't worried they might hurt you?"

"Of course I was worried, a little. A bunch of idiots with badges and weapons harassing you is not something I'd recommend if you want a relaxing evening. But I can take care of myself. And those nitwits were on their way out and they knew it, wouldn't have badges much longer. Half would be gone less than a year later. Copbots would replace them all within three. Their last gasp to intimidate me was more pathetic than scary. Anyway, look, I'm not here to dwell on the past or the outside."

"Why are you here?" Margoria asked.

"I have questions for you about my current case. What do you know about Sannien?"

Margoria lowered Annie before asking, "Saney? Has something happened to him?"

"He's fine. I'm here investigating some business irregularities, nothing very serious. Just checking in with people who know him well."

"That certainly isn't me," she said.

"Didn't you date him for five months?"

"I did. I thought I knew him well. But obviously that wasn't the case, because here I am still stuck teaching ventriloquism."

"They say that teaching is a calling," Harken said.

Her pedagogical enthusiasm from a moment earlier had disappeared. "It isn't calling me. I'm not supposed to be teaching. I'm supposed to be up on a stage entertaining people and basking in applause. I'm Margoria Magnificent."

"And Sannien has something to do with this?"

---

[43] It sounded suspiciously similar to the chanting of "Daarryyll, Daarryyll, Daarryyll," which in ancient times was used to taunt an athlete in a now-obscure sport. According to documentary evidence, the game consisted mainly of players standing around and spitting.

"He's a huge influenceleb. He has influence. It's right there in the job title. He could have shared my vids, told people to watch them. He could have told that manager of his, that stupid fake general, to get me a show of my own."

Harken corrected her. "He's a fake general major."

"Is that even a real thing? Are there general majors in armies or something?"

"I don't think so, no."

"Well, whatever, Saney refused to help me. And that's after I gave him all of this." She indicated her slinky shimmering dark blue dress with a wave of her hand.[44]

"That's why you were dating him, so he could help your career?"

"Absolutely not! It was love, for me."

"Right."

"No, really, it was. I fell hard for that boy. I wanted to be his ever since that first date, when I took him to the Treeseeum to see the teak trees used to make the best dummies, like my Annie. But yes, I thought along the way I'd become a celeb myself. Ventriloquists are very popular these days. It wouldn't have been that hard, you know. He could have helped a little. A mention here, some enthusiasm there. Instead, he pretended my act didn't even exist. Whenever I brought it up, he accused me of using him to further my career, said I didn't really love him."

"And that's why you broke it off?" Harken asked.

"No," Magnificent said, sadness creeping into her voice. "That's not why I broke it off. I never broke it off. I would have stayed anyway. I told you, I fell hard for that boy. But he found someone he liked better. That stupid juggler!"

"Juggler?"

"I don't want to talk about him. He took Saney away from me." She started to cry.

---

[44] Maybe the dress wasn't even Sannien's size. That would explain why she still had it.

"Ms. Magnificent," Harken started, but he didn't get to finish.

She had picked up Annie the dummy and, in character, it said quite firmly, just inches from Harken's face, "She said she doesn't want to talk about him! Please leave. You've upset us. Now!"

The ventriloquism was convincing, passionate. She really was talented, and as we left Dummy Academy like Annie requested, I couldn't help thinking that Sannien should have done more to help Margoria Magnificent's career even if she did call him Saney.

5

Two men wearing sport coats were waiting for us outside Dummy Academy. We knew right away they worked for Tommy Ten-Toes, because they wore sport coats and said they worked for Tommy Ten-Toes. Their boss wanted to speak to us and we should go with them. If you aren't familiar with Ten-Toes, I should first tell you that the actual number of toes he possessed and how he got his name were both subjects of much conjecture [45] among his loyal henchpeople. Suffice it to say that most theories concluded that whatever the truth was, it was wise to do what Tommy Ten-Toes wanted.

Harken seemed to agree. He didn't object to accompanying the two men to pay Ten-Toes a visit. I expected him to look at his watch and say we didn't have time for this because minutes

---

[45] This is explained in detail in the chronicle of our first case, but I'm not going to keep telling you to read *The Great American Deception*. I have my pride.

counted, but instead we went with them. When we were on the magnashuttle, I asked him if his watch was broken. It was an older model—borderline ancient—and I'd subtly suggested several times in the past eight days that he might want to consider upgrading to a new one. A broken watch could be the reason minutes didn't count at the moment. He assured me that his watch was functioning just fine. "Ten-Toes wants to see me just as I'm beginning to investigate a case? His men are waiting for me when I finish talking to a possible suspect? Those could be coincidences."

"And since you're not a big believer in coincidences, you think this isn't one and Ten-Toes has something to do with our case." I deduced this from the question marks at the end of two of his sentences—I was getting good at being a detective.

"Yes, could be. Maybe we'll learn something relevant when we talk to Ten-Toes. Maybe we won't. Either way, there's plenty of time before the party tonight."

The shuttle was at 83% capacity, and Harken was sitting on a bench along one side. I wasn't sitting anywhere because I am not designed to sit. Don't worry! My legs weren't tired at all for the same reason my feet weren't. Sport-coat guys were standing even though there were empty seats—maybe they weren't allowed to sit while on duty. They weren't interested in conversation, either. Some henchpeople don't add much to the story, but fortunately Harken and I had enough to talk about without them.

Could Margoria Magnificent be the blackmailer? Sure, why not, Harken said. There's no telling what a spurned lover might do, especially when there's career envy and resentment thrown in. And after that last bit from her dummy Annie, well, we might also have questions about Margoria's psychological stability. She could be involved. The problem was we still knew so little about the case. What was the information being used to blackmail Sannien? What were the blackmailer's demands? Harken often thought out loud with questions about our current case. It was one of his more endearing quirks.

I told him I was sorry that Margoria Magnificent became so upset, because I would have liked to talk more with Annie. Yes, I knew she was a dummy and her voice was coming from someone else. However, the same could be said for Al the griddle pan. And the argumatons. Could it be said for me? Was I as different from Annie or Al as I thought? Sometimes I wasn't so sure. I didn't have a slinky blue dress or know how to make pancakes, had no identifiable speech chip, but I *had* been programmed at some point. Even though I was only eight days old and had no memories of my creation before then, it stood to reason that someone had programmed me. I thought I chose my words and actions for myself, but how could I know if I didn't?

Frank Harken said this was a little deep for a casual shuttle ride on only our eight-day-iversary. He was no philosopher—this stuff was a bit above his paygrade—but if it made me feel any better, plenty of humans had the same question about themselves. How could anyone know?

Maroon Neighborhood 261 was a central magnashuttle hub. Crowds were thicker than throng density as we pushed through molk shoving their way toward the platforms. We followed the sport-coat guys up to the next level and passed through the second largest food court in Western Region Eleven. There were ninety-six eateries and fifteen snack kiosks arranged in a double-decker crescent. Sunlight filtered through atrium glass, harmful rays removed, beneficial vitamin D enhanced, casting shadows from palm trees across a substantial portion of the 16,872 diners enjoying a casual meal and doing their civic duty. The lunchtime trial was underway, a rare murder case.

The Great American was great, but its inhabitants were not perfect. They occasionally fought, stole, cheated, vandalized, and generally behaved like human beings. The punishment for such behavior usually involved restitution to those harmed and restrictions on the perpetrator's access to Great American amenities. A few months without being allowed to buy shoes could serve as powerful corrective rehabilitation. Especially violent behavior was rare in part because of the peacegrid, a real-time vid stream from the digi-contacts of millions of volunteers. GAS saw whatever these millions saw, which helped keep the crime rate low and catch criminals.

Even with the peacegrid, however, Great American people were people, and sometimes committed terrible violence, even killed each other, usually in the heat of the moment,[46] when gripped by the passion of a shoe riot for example. If found guilty by a food court, criminals with that kind of temper could be sentenced to adrenosnooze implantation, which caused them to need a nap whenever they got too worked up. It was quite effective at preventing future violent behavior and also functioned as a deterrent before the fact, since adrenosnooze kept people from staying awake for even the peaceful, pleasurable kind of excitement, a fate most wanted to avoid. For the rare psychopaths who couldn't be deterred by the peacegrid nor forced to be nonviolent by adrenosnooze, for those who killed in cold blood[47] without fear of consequences, there was exile.

That's what the man on trial at the food court was facing if convicted. He had been dubbed the "Happy Birthday Killer" by news reports, because a killing isn't interesting unless it has a snappy name. The prosecutor told the dining jury of thousands that, a week earlier, the accused had killed seven people in the Rib Shack in Green Neighborhood 412. His motive had been simple. He didn't like the birthday song employees sang to customers who were there celebrating birthdays. The waiters in their matching Rib Shack shirts always gathered round the table and sang,

Birthday, Birthday, Birthday, Birthday, Birthday,
Birthday, Birthday, Birthday, Birthday, Birthday,
Eat some ribs!

---

[46] Excessive heat could make people quite irritable.

[47] A heated moment, cooler blood—people liked to blame violence on temperature. The truth is, though, even a killer's cold blood was the same temperature as anyone else's, approximately 98.6 degrees Fahrenheit unless the killer had a fever.

The defendant was highly critical of the song. He was appalled that it was not the traditional "Happy Birthday" from his youth and irate that the word *Happy* didn't even get a single mention. He'd been tormented by the lyrics ever since his birthday three weeks earlier, when he'd gone by himself to Rib Shack to celebrate the special day. The waiters had gathered round and sang their birthday song to him, then left him alone. As he was eating ribs on his birthday, he realized they never wished him a happy birthday, and right there and then he decided that the Rib Shack birthday song was an atrocity that had caused the death of Great American tradition.

Two weeks later, after recording his 42,398-word largely incoherent manifesto, he printed a homemade gun, entered Rib Shack, and waited for someone to have a birthday. Besides the manifesto, there was peacegrid vid of the shooting from eight different witnesses and victims. It didn't take the jury long to convict. Their chicken nuggets were still mildly warm when they delivered the verdict. Justice had prevailed, and the Happy Birthday Killer would be exiled within hours.

The Outside Experience was under construction. Sport-coat guys entered, and we followed, passing under the massive three-dimensional neon sign that remained unlit. Inside were a handful[48] of other sport-coat guys and Tommy Ten-Toes. He wore a black lightning-striped suit, which was like a pinstriped suit if the thick white pinstripes cut jagged, vertical lightning bolts. The effect was of white lightning with black background, or black lightning with white background, depending on how the light hit the suit and what your eyes focused on at any moment. Since I didn't have eyes, this didn't bother me. Humans, though, were likely to be distracted, almost hypnotized, their eyes drawn down the suit and away from Ten-Toes' face. That was fine with them, because looking too long at

---

[48] Not literally. They were regular size.

his face was unsettling. He had a way of meeting your eyes even while seeming to be staring off to the side.

Construction workers, fabulists, and authentiscapers were everywhere, trailed by schlepbots schlepping supplies and tools. It was a tremendous space, 440 yards by 803 yards. Cranebots were putting up curved walls near the center, reached the top of the fifty-foot ceiling. The director of the project was talking to Ten-Toes. She was a leading authentiscaper, had been in charge of the design of the twenty-first-century metropolitan habitat at the Great American Zoo (which, by the way, I really loved—the cockroach apartment was exceptionally informative. It wasn't my favorite part of the zoo, but how could it be when I had already seen nursing tiger cubs in the jungle habitat? Still, it was top-notch). Ten-Toes finished explaining something to his project director and approached us. Did I mention he was wearing a sling around his right arm? I should mention that because it's possible I had something to do with it. [49]

"Detective, to what do I owe the pleasure?"

"Ten-Toes, you sent for me."

"I didn't know if you'd come."

"Does anyone refuse an invitation from Tommy Ten-Toes?"

"No, no one does. But no one else is walking around with such a capable coffee machine. Which for some reason is wearing a hat." His left hand patted his right arm in its sling as he nodded at me.

"I hope your arm is feeling better," I said.

"Not even broken," Ten-Toes said. "A few more days, it'll be good as new."

Harken was not in the mood for chatting. "How'd you find me? What do you have to do with my case?"

Ten-Toes was disappointed. "Detective, we're making small talk. You should try it some time. It could be a step forward in our friendship."

---

[49] A reminder about my chronicle of a past case could go here, but I already told you that I have my pride and am done telling you to read it. Please don't even look at this footnote.

"When did you get all touchy-feely? Small talk? Friendship? That doesn't sound like the feared crime boss Tommy Ten-Toes I know. And I don't need more friends." (This made sense, of course. He already had me.) "What's your game,[50] anyway? Were your men tailing me?"

"No. One of my gluten dealers saw you. The match was relayed automatically. I like to keep track of my friends as well as my enemies."

"You're dealing gluten now? I thought you said you were going straight."

"Don't be a moron. I never said I was going straight. Besides, gluten isn't illegal. I could open a store and sell it off shelves if I wanted to, but teens prefer to make clandestine purchases. We can charge twice as much selling that way. Totally legal side money. I told you that the rackets is no way to make a living in here. Entertainment is where it's at. That's why I'm opening The Outside Experience in just a few weeks. It's going to be even more popular than Win-Fall.[51] People in here just can't get enough of the outside."

"That's because they haven't seen the real thing."

"Mostly, but you'd be surprised. Even new residents, some inside only a year, are clamoring for the outside. Nostalgia businesses are making a killing all over the Great American."

"So what's this place gonna do, give molk the thrill of empty market shelves?"

"Have a little imagination, detective. You have to envision authentiscaping indistinguishable from the real thing. A city block, a scene right out of the Portland Sourdough Rebellion, copbots battling protestors. Our customers will experience what it was like to really be there. Every detail. They'll have to sign waivers first, of course, and show proof of insurance. And wear

---

[50] I hoped it was chess. I had yet to find a worthy opponent.

[51] A high-stakes-casino-game-show-all-you-can-eat buffet with forty-five locations throughout the Great American. It was a central part of the Ten-Toes business empire and had gambling activities like Argumania, which, by the way, I had found to be quite enjoyable.

helmets and padding. The copbots will treat them like real protestors."

"You're gonna have copbots in here, in the Great American? They'll allow that?"

"Not real ones. Simulations. But people won't be able to tell the difference. We're also putting in a mountain region drone attack. Not everything will be so dramatic, though. I expect the caught-in-a-rainstorm-without-an-umbrella experience to be very popular, as well. And we'll have a whole section devoted to twentieth-century adventures. It'll include a parallel-parking challenge—circle a city block in a 1985 five-speed Plymouth Turismo with a wonky clutch looking for a spot and then we let you find the smallest one. No cameras or robot assist, not even power steering.[52] And there'll be a corner store where people try sending a fax but the receiving end is always busy."[53]

"People are gonna pay for this?"

"People already have. Deposits for bachelorette parties, corporate outings, birthdays. Parallel parking is booked for two months."

"You really have come a long way from hijacking trucks."

"I had nothing to do with that. I told you, detective, I'm an upstanding, law-abiding business mogul now. Just a peaceful entrepreneur. I'm not the old Tommy Ten-Toes you remember from the outside. As long as you don't cross me."

"And I told you I've left the past in the past where it belongs, so if that's where the Ten-Toes I knew is, okay, fine. But that doesn't make us friends. Come on—why'd you send for me?"

Ten-Toes snapped his fingers and a sport-coat guy brought him a drink, bourbon on the rocks. I sensed that Harken was working up a thirst of his own and handed him a delicious coffee. The two stood there enjoying their beverages for a moment.

---

[52] This could be an especially difficult task for many Great American residents, since only those who'd lived on the outside had ever driven an actual car.

[53] No, I don't know what this means, either.

"Look, detective, I'm not in the habit of having to ask for favors. Usually I tell someone to do something and they do it."

"You want a favor? From me?"

"Yes, as a matter of fact, I do. I happen to have a lot invested in the influenceleb Sannien. You'll be at his party tonight."

"How do you know that?"

"Like I said, I keep track of my friends as well as my enemies. Sannien will be promoting The Outside Experience all year, a big part of our marketing plan. So, you can understand it's more than a little troubling that I've heard through the grapevine someone's going to kill him tonight."

"The grapevine? Doesn't sound like the most reliable source," Harken said.

"It's served me pretty well over the years. But no, we haven't been able to confirm it. My people have asked around."

"And what do you want me to do?"

"You'll be there, so you can make sure he doesn't get killed."

"Ten-Toes, I'm a detective, not a bodyguard. Why don't your people do it?"

"Oh, I'll have people there as well. But none of them have quite the capacity of your coffee machine here. The two of you can make sure no harm comes to Sannien and find out if anyone's really trying to kill him. If the threat is real, you'll give me their name. I'll take care of it from there."

"Now I get it. This offer of friendship is really about Arjay helping you out."

"Well, detective, he was impressive the last time I saw him." Ten-Toes made a slight movement with his slinged arm.

It was nice to be acknowledged. "Don't worry, Mr. Ten-Toes, I'm on the case."

Harken gave me a look that said, *We're partners—you don't accept side deals, especially not from former crime bosses with whom I have a long, acrimonious history.*

I corrected myself. "That is, if my partner agrees."

Harken reluctantly agreed. "We'll do what we can to keep Sannien safe. That's all I can promise. We're not handing over any names to you."

Ten-Toes smiled, an unsettling sight. "Very well, detective. We'll deal with that when the time comes."

My partner was annoyed. Perhaps befuddled. Tommy Ten-Toes being civil, bordering on friendly, was unexpected. Why couldn't we ever get a simple case? Most detectives had one client per case at a time. We already had three for this one, though it was not yet clear what exactly the case was about. General Major Driver wanted us to find out who was black-mailing Sannien, despite not being able to tell us anything else about it. Nutella wanted us to make sure no one got killed at Sannien's party, but only had a vague notion that someone might get killed and her only source of information was something very reliable called *chatter*. Tommy Ten-Toes was more specific, wanted us to prevent Sannien from being killed at the same party, and his source was something even more precise called *a grapevine*. None of this satisfied a detective looking for actual evidence. We still had a couple of leads to chase down before the evening's big event and Harken hoped we'd learn something worthwhile, but he didn't sound optimistic. Fortunately, I was optimistic enough for both of us and then some. "Don't worry, Frank Harken. I have full confidence in your detecting prowess."

My assurance was small consolation as we walked through Bronze Neighborhood 290, passing stores for shoes, blouses, playglobes, peanut-free imitation peanut products, sports memorabilia, jeans, holo trainers, witty T-shirts, and mini-golf equipment. Along the way, there were kiosks and fountains and a man selling pickles on sticks out of a large barrel. You might think it odd to see someone standing in a barrel, submerged to his torso in brine, waving pickles on sticks and shouting "Dill! Sweet! Bread and butter! Candied! Half sour!" But that's how artisanal pickles were typically sold in the Great American and people were quite accustomed to it. Don't worry! Pickle peddlers wore extra-thick protective wetsuits and goggles that could withstand the strongest pickle juice. Some sold pickles in a less traditional way, at stores and deli counters, but true connoisseurs wouldn't buy from anyone besides a submerged pickle peddler. The truest of the true connoisseurs often home-pickled and could be quite snobbish about any purchased, even the classic submerged peddler artisanal variety.

Up ahead was the bronze roller coaster, one of the neighborhood's main attractions. The central path widened to make room for it, stores on either side replaced by smaller carnival booths where people could have their weight guessed, their cards read, their face painted, their forehead tattooed. With its twenty-three loops and six corkscrews, the last one through a ring of fire, the bronze coaster had a line winding all the way around the back and past the cotton candy vendor. Parents and younger kids opted for the merry-go-round, riding on animated horses, giraffes, lions, unicorns, dragons, griffins, brontosauri, humpback whales, and oversized squirrels. It was nearly 4:00, the angle of the setting sun through atrium windows prompting lights to gradually brighten all around the neighborhood.

Teenagers with flashing hair weaves and glowing fingernails were everywhere. Many had tails, of course. Those with attached-belt-harness mechanical tails tended to hang out with like-tailed friends. It was fun to make the tails dance to the rhythm of accordion-rap-ska carnival music, which all but drowned out the screams of people whipping though the ring of fire on the bronze coaster. Those teens with actual bioengineered fleshy eel-tails also tended to self-segregate. Sadly, the Great American had a long way to go to achieve teen tail harmony. We had just cleared a group of them beyond the coaster when we saw our first gang altercation. Thankfully, it wasn't between tail factions. They had a bad-enough reputation for fighting each other already.

No, this dispute was between Red Cappers and Face Maskers, two gangs that had been around since before the Great American, starting on the outside. Red Cappers hated Face Maskers, and Face Maskers hated Red Cappers, and the hate had been passed down through the generations. Maybe it was a lot like the Hatfields and McCoys, if the Hatfields and McCoys wore red caps and face masks and instead of Kentucky and West Virginia lived in the Great American and also weren't related to each other. It actually wasn't at all like the Hatfields and McCoys, when you thought about it, except for the hating each other for generations. That part was very H&Mc. Maybe it was more like the Crips and Bloods, if one gang wore red caps and one gang wore face masks and they all lived in the shiny, spectacular Great American and their violent conflicts consisted mainly of shouting and calling each other *snowflakes*. Otherwise, not so much.

The shouting soon escalated to louder shouting and the use of mean words like *cuckburger*, *magadipspittle*, and *hockenbougie*. The people yelling them didn't know what these words meant, but they did know people hearing it were offended, and that was what mattered. Like the meaning of these words and so much else from the old days outside, the origins of the hostility between Red Cappers and Face Maskers had been, if not lost to history, at least misdirected by it. You might say they were

obscured by time and shrouded in myth if you talked like that.[54]
The Red Cappers and Face Maskers yelled louder still and were
on the verge of engaging in a real slugfest[55] when seven GAS
officers arrived and positioned themselves between the two
groups.

Wearing their usual neon yellow and red uniforms and
violent sneers, the GAS officers raised their stunners. They
loved to stun fighting teens. And drunk and disorderly adults.
And shoplifters. And Frank Harken, if they could come up with
a good excuse. (They sometimes could.) Fortunately, stunners
only gave people a sudden burst of temporary sleep, accompanied occasionally by profuse drooling. It was a little sloppy
but a vast improvement over law-enforcement tactics on the
outside, where the imposed sleep could be permanent and quite
bloody. In this case, much to the disappointment of the GAS
officers, stunning was not necessary. The tough teens on both
sides backed off at the sight of raised weapons and the two gangs
went their separate ways. There would be no hauling them down
to a GAS station holding cell to sleep it off.

I was happy the fight was prevented, because Red Cappers
and Face Maskers looked like they weren't very good at it. If we
wanted to see fighting, a better option would be the kickboxing
clowns in the ring just up ahead putting on an exhibition bout
for an appreciative audience. It wasn't easy getting those big
clown shoes off the ground for a jump kick, but these clowns
were no jokers when it came to personal combat. Even in full
costume—makeup, bright wig, water-squirting flower on lapel—
they put on quite a martial arts show. However, minutes seemed
to count now, since Harken said we hadn't come all the way to
Bronze Neighborhood 290 to watch bozos battle. We weren't
there to ride the bronze roller coaster, or get our weight guessed
or forehead tattooed. No, we weren't even there to buy one of
those artisanal pickles. We were there to see the juggler.

---

[54] It's not how I would phrase it.
[55] Not the kind involving real slugs.

Even more popular than the bronze coaster was the juggler. Or, as he called himself, The Juggler. It's true there were other jugglers in the Great American. Thousands of them. But they were lowercase jugglers. There was only one uppercase juggler known as The Juggler and he was headlining at the Pentagon in Bronze Neighborhood 290. The Pentagon was a five-sided stage with bleachers all around. It was the last attraction in the neighborhood before you entered Aqua Neighborhood 278. Unless you entered from Aqua Neighborhood 278, in which case it was the first attraction. Great American geography could be confusing.

All around, from outside the small arena, you could only see the backs of bleachers. There was a path between bleachers at each of the Pentagon's corners. A security guard stopped us—the show was almost over and no one was permitted to enter during the performance. It was distracting to the audience and the performer and with an act like The Juggler's, distractions could be dangerous. She whispered that she'd let us in to talk to him when the show was over. Harken and I had a clear view of The Juggler from the path and could see behind him a full section of twenty rows of bleachers. Everywhere astonished faces gaped at his remarkable display of dexterity and daring.

The Juggler's electric blue unitard highlighted a physique that had exceeded perfection at least 6,834 pushups ago. His muscles had muscles, yet he wasn't over muscled. All was symmetry, smoothness, lightness. He was barefoot and seemed to glide in tiny increments about the center of the padded stage as the objects of his otherworldly focus sailed around and around. It had been thought for many years that no more than fourteen balls could be juggled at one time, but that was before the advent of lens-brain connection that had led to shattered records in so many areas. Still, even with the technological assistance, what The Juggler was doing was unheard of.[56]

---

[56] Until now, at least, since I'm telling you.

He was juggling, with his hands, a rotation of sixteen mini vibesaws, a feat more difficult than juggling balls because he had to catch and throw them by their handles. Meanwhile, simultaneously (*meanwhile* and *simultaneously* are redundant, but only redundancy can convey just how impressive this was), with the U-pipe strapped to his back he was juggling fourteen balls. The balls fell out of the air into one end of the U and were launched back up through the other end. Can you picture it? Sixteen mini vibesaws, each one capable of slicing a hand off with the slightest misjudgment, spinning in the air and being thrown back up into perfect position to be caught and thrown again. The Juggler's hands were a blur. Meanwhile, at the same time (which also means simultaneously), he had to keep track of the balls, fourteen of them, and get himself into position to catch each one in the correct side of the back U-pipe so it could be launched into the air a millisecond later. You can't picture it, can you? Humans have such limited capacity for visualization.

After seventy-three seconds, the coup de grâce (no one was killed, but it was very dramatic and very final). The Juggler caught two vibesaws and leaped out of the way. Fourteen balls were left to fall to the padded floor of the stage. Fourteen vibesaws were left to fall as well, and each sliced a ball in half as it reached the stage. The roaring cheers didn't start immediately, because at first no one in the audience believed what they had seen. Tricks and simulations were common in the Great American—so much of what amazed people was virtual. This was not and the people knew it. After a collective silent gasp, the ovation was thundering, deservedly so. It was the single most impressive physical act I'd seen a human perform in my entire eight days of existence, requiring reflexes and calculations that should have been impossible, were impossible for anyone besides The Juggler. The lens-brain connection helped, made the impossible possible, yet only for him. He was a singular talent.

I could easily do the same, but to be fair I wasn't a human— my reflexes and calculations weren't constrained by organic limitations like eyes or a brain. Also, I had four arms, which is twice as many as The Juggler had. Still, his was a glorious performance, and I clapped with all four hands. Even Frank Harken clapped with genuine enthusiasm, and that was saying something—as you probably realize by now, he hated almost everything.

We didn't go backstage because the stage had no back, being a pentagon surrounded by bleachers on all sides. At the end of The Juggler's performance, the floor opened beneath him and he fell through, a dramatic exit that made the cheering crowd cheer louder. After the applause ebbed and finally people filtered out of the Pentagon, we were led to a cellar door at the base of the stage. Harken knocked, but there was no answer, so he opened the door and we descended the stairs. Don't worry! My fourteen strategically positioned wheels had no difficulty navigating stairs.[57]

Beneath the stage was a fully furnished apartment, and we found ourselves in a living room facing The Juggler, who sat in a recliner and slurped from a hydration tube connected to a pouch on the end table next to him. Juggling the way he did depleted essential vitamins and minerals and frequently re-plenishing fluids was a key component of his regimen. He gestured at the loveseat opposite his chair. "I hear you want to talk to me. Have a seat, gentlemen."

I was not especially gentle nor a man, and besides, without legs or buttocks, having a seat wasn't an option. Harken, however, possessing all the necessary body parts, sat. I handed him a coffee.

"So, Juggler—" Harken said before being interrupted.

The Juggler corrected him. "That's *The* Juggler."

"Your first name is *The*?"

"I don't have a first name. It's just one name: The Juggler."

---

[57] I could also ski if the occasion called for it. And wait till you find out about my tank treads.

Harken didn't generally have strong opinions about the names people gave themselves. "I'll call you whatever you want, though it's a little wordy. Every time anyone says your name, they have to put a *The* in front of it. Not very efficient."

"The *The* is important," The Juggler said, and there could be no arguing with that. "How can I help you, Detective Harken?"

"I'm working on a case related to Sannien. I hear the two of you are currently an item."

The Juggler laughed. "*An item*? What is this, 1980?"

Harken did sometimes fall into old-timey lingo. He might have watched too many ancient detective movies.

"Okay, not an *item*. What do you want to call it? Dating? Together? A couple?"

The Juggler wasn't eager to define it, preferred to keep things up in the air. "We see each other sometimes."

"How'd you two meet?"

The Juggler still slurped from his hydration tube. "He was in the front row at my show a few months ago and couldn't take his eyes off me. Can you blame him? I *am* The Juggler. During the show he streamed part of my performance to his followers. Normally, we don't allow that, but when an influenceleb like Sane wants to promote you for free, you let him. What am I saying? There are no influencelebs like Sane! Before I knew it, I had a new manager and got signed for bigger shows, landed this gig at the Pentagon just a few weeks later."

"Can I assume the new manager is General Major Driver?"

"You can."

"How's that going?"

"He said he has big plans for me, a headliner tour of the whole Great American. I'm obviously going to be a star."

"Obviously," Harken agreed.

"Anyway, what's this all about? Is Sane in some kind of trouble?"

"No. There's been a vague threat against him—nothing serious—and I'm just seeing if anyone knows anything that could help me figure it out. Do you live here? Under the stage?"

"Only when I'm performing at the Pentagon, for the next two weeks this time around. It's too much of a hassle to go back and forth to a housing unit in the residential district. I perform every four hours all through the day and night—the crowds never stop in this neighborhood. I have to catch sleep between shows. It's soundproof, you know."

"So you won't be at Sannien's party tonight?"

"Sadly, no. Such is the life of a performance artist. The show must go on. But I'll be there in spirit."[58]

"Can you think of anyone who might have a grudge against Sannien, anyone who doesn't like him?"

"Detective, have you met Sane?"

"No, not yet. I will tonight at the party."

"When you do, you'll understand this better: no one likes him."

"No one? Aren't you dating—that is, seeing him some-times?"

"I am. It might even be getting serious. But that doesn't mean I like him."

Harken didn't know what to say to that. Great American relationships could be confusing. With my partner speechless, I took over the interview. "I just want to say, Mr. The Juggler, that your juggling was impressive." I pointed to the bucket of yellow balls next to the loveseat. "Are these your practice balls?"

He admired my hat, then spoke in a condescending tone. "You can give it a try if you like. Bots don't have the dexterity to juggle more than a couple, though."

I grabbed thirty-one balls from the bucket and threw them into the air in quicker-than-quick succession. With three of my hands moving too fast to see, I juggled the balls, a feat not even The Juggler could match. Despite the low ceiling, which made the task especially challenging, I could have continued indefi-nitely, or longer. With my fourth hand, more accurately, a finger on my fourth hand, I gave him a Mutombo finger wag, the uni-versal gesture for, "Oh no you don't!"

---

[58] Ooh, magic!

74

Sheeple were everywhere. I counted seventy-two as we entered Violet Neighborhood 315. Days could go by without a sighting—I'd only seen one before. But the weeklong sheeple convention at the Baroque Center had attracted sheeple from all across the Great American. They wore no shirts over their fluffy wool torsos. Self-grown sweaters were the latest micro-fad—it hadn't caught on in large numbers, partly because temperatures in the Great American were steady and comfortable and there was no need to wear a permanent sweater. *Sweater* was an apt name because if you wore one, you'd certainly sweat.[59] Sheeple could trim their upper-body wool to keep themselves a little cooler, but most did not. The whole point of being a sheeple was displaying the wonderful, fluffy wool that was as much a part of

---

[59] Unless you were a coffeebot like me, without sweat or other glands. But in that case it's unlikely you'd wear a sweater anyway. The most you might wear is a hat, if you also happened to be a detective.

your body as the hair on your head. The fluffier and woolier, the better.

Body modification was popular in the Great American, went far beyond the until-today rare sheeple sighting. People liked to accessorize and upgrade their crude matter with piercings, tails, legstensions, sculpted faces, rushtaches, bejeweled teeth, body hair implants, animated tattoos, and of course omnipresent colored lenses that connected so many to each other. In recent years, controversial and expensive melanin adjustments even allowed people to decide how light or dark they wanted their skin to be on a given day. And new developments in skin color were already being advertised. Soon it would be possible to tint yourself in any RGB combination. Somewhere in the Great American was at least one frail tough guy who would tell people they wouldn't like him when he's angry, before turning green.

Past the sheeple convention and three mini-golf courses (Greek myths, industrial accidents, pirates), and around the corner from a Drink or Swim, was Collectors Row. One of the joys of living in the Great American was getting a good deal and the more good deals you got, the more you needed a place to keep the things you got a good deal on. Even the biggest and fanciest housing units on residential district level fifteen had less space than many homes did outside in the old days. And housing units on lower residential levels had less space still. What did you do if you liked lamps but only had room for one in your housing unit? (It doesn't matter that all housing units had overhead recessed lighting and lamps weren't necessary. *Necessary* had nothing to do with people liking lamps.) An option was to simply own one lamp, but that was clearly ludicrous. What was the point of living in the Great American if you could only own one lamp?

Collectors Row solved this existential dilemma by providing hundreds of thousands[60] of storage units with good overhead (non-lamp) lighting and generous shelving right in the shopping district. If you owned fifty-three lamps, you could visit them whenever you wanted. Maybe you'd bring a friend to see them. Possibly a fellow lamp connoisseur. You could greet the lamps aloud if talking to inanimate objects were the sort of thing you did. It wasn't all about lamps, however. Only 12.61% of Collectors Row space was devoted to decorative lighting. People collected all manner of other valuable collectibles that they didn't have room for in their housing units, and any time of day or night you could find someone at Collectors Row visiting their cherished collection of crystal vases, kaleidoscopes, frog figurines, antique furniture, porcelain dolls, paintings, action figures, and, most popular of all, shoes. The storage units were stacked four high and ten across and extended into the distance as far as the eye could see.[61] When we passed the first 1,480 units, I told Harken to follow me and we headed left to a shortcut toward the residential district elevators.

"Dogs! Dogs! Dogs dogs dogs dogs!" My enthusiasm barometer indicated dangerous levels, but I couldn't help myself. "Dogs!"

"Arjay, calm down! I thought you said this was a shortcut. Why are we at a Great American Dog Park?"

"Dogs!" I shouted.

We were at a Great American Dog Park. Maybe you've deduced that already from Harken's question. Or from my

---

[60] Collectors Row had 553 locations throughout the Great American, but faced stiff competition from up-and-coming businesses Storagevilletown, Hoarder's Hideaway, and Keep Your Stuff Here.

[61] Not the human eye. That would mean Collectors Row went on for miles, which isn't realistic even for the Great American. And certainly not the eye of an eagle or hawk, which could see even farther. What do you mean, "What kind of eye, then?" There is no eye. It's just an expression.

shouting, "Dogs!" (If so, good detective work.) I was having difficulty controlling my enthusiasm. You probably figured that out already, too. (You're a natural.) I'm not doing a good job of telling this part. The presence of sixty-eight dogs was making it hard to focus and even now, simply recalling it, I'm overwhelmed with enthusiasm. Dogs![62]

The Great American Dog Park was a park for dogs, as the name implied. If you didn't know that people in the Great American had dogs, perhaps because it has not been mentioned before, now you know. It should have been obvious, though, a simple matter of deductive reasoning, really. The Great American is widely acknowledged as the greatest civilization to ever exist. Its vast variety of mini-golf proves that. And a civilization can't be great if people don't want to live there. Do people want to live where there are no dogs? No, they don't. Ergo, the Great American had to have dogs. And have dogs it did.

As you recently learned in the description of Collectors Row, most housing units in the residential district weren't very large and gave dogs little room to exercise. In addition, the shopping district was often crowded at or beyond throng density, not an ideal setting for leisurely dog walking. People needed someplace for their dogs to run and frolic. Fortunately, Great American Dog Parks were often located conveniently near residential district elevator banks. So, I wasn't lying when I told Harken that this was a shortcut.

"We talked about this already," Harken said. "We're not getting a dog."

"I don't know what you're referring to." Though still elevated, my enthusiasm had returned to a manageable level.

"Arjay, just this morning you asked again if we could get a puppy. For the thousandth time."

"That's a ridiculous exaggeration. I have only asked if we could get a puppy thirty-nine times."

"In the past eight days."

"Well, I'm sorry for not existing before then."

---

[62] See what I mean?

"I don't want to hear another word about dogs or puppies or pooches or any of the other canine synonyms you've been bombarding me with the last week. We'll go through this dog park because the elevators are on the other side and we have a case to work on, but you are not to make a scene. Do you understand me?"

I didn't appreciate being spoken to like a child, which I conveyed to Harken by saying, "I don't appreciate being spoken to like a child." Then I entered the Great American Dog Park and he followed, shaking his head behind me as if I didn't know that was exactly what he was doing.

Sixty-one of the sixty-eight dogs were some variety of doodle or poo. Most dogs were these days. There were minis, smalls, in-betweens, mediums, standards, larges, jumbos, and other sizes people hadn't come up with names for. The artificial grass cushioned doggy knees as they ran and leapt and tumbled. Doggy obstacles like ramps and pipe tunnels gave the doggos plenty of opportunities to explore and express their adventurous spirits. Dogs being dogs, some expressed their spirits more excrementally, but that was no cause for concern. Patrolling poopbots scooped up any messes and insta-steamed the grass to remove stains and germs. Tennis ball launchers and squirrel-bots kept the pooches occupied while dog owners drank hard seltzer at the Great American Dog Park bar.

Sadly, we passed through without incident. I was hoping to make some canine friends, but the dogs were not interested in me, might have been too busy chasing the squirrelbots all over. Possibly they were deliberately avoiding me, put off by my shouting, "Dogs! Dogs! Dogs!" as my enthusiasm built back up.

When we exited the dog park, Harken offered a compromise. "You're obviously too excitable to have a puppy. Maybe if you show some self-control the rest of the day, we can talk about getting a pet rock."

The first five levels of the residential district were stationary. This means they didn't move, not that they were fancy embossed paper used for sending letters in olden times. Housing units on levels six and above glided along tracks, slowly and smoothly traversing the continent and the Great American. On level eight, doors on either side of the corridor moved away from us, not quite fast enough to create the illusion that we were walking in slow motion. Still, Harken paused for a moment before knocking when he got to the platform outside the housing unit's door, as was advisable to avoid disorientation.

The door slid open with barely a hiss and we were met by an extraordinarily ordinary-looking young woman who did not appear to have a tail, sculpted face, blinking hair, or even eyes that changed colors. Her jeans were fashionably ripped at the knees and her witty T-shirt displayed the hilarious words, *Stop Reading Me!* She recognized my partner immediately. "Detective Frank Harken!"

"That's my name." He didn't tell her not to wear it out, because names are not material and can't really be worn out by overuse.

Jane Smith invited us in. She told us she was a big fan of the detective, had studied his most famous cases. The Beguiling Mystery of the Missing Necklace. The Unexpected Incident of the Heirloom Tomato. The Strange Times Those Three Other Things Happened That No One Else Could Figure Out. Her housing unit was standard for level eight, two rooms and a small but full kitchen. The living room was modest, had a mere ninety-inch television embedded in the wall, but we weren't in any position to look down on it, since Harken lived on level six, a lower level with a smaller television and only a kitchenette. Yes, he was a famous detective, with well-known necklace and tomato cases, but that hadn't made him wealthy.[63]

"Ms. Smith, I'd like to ask you some questions about Sannien."

---

[63] The richest thing about him was the coffee he'd been drinking for the past eight days.

"Sannien?"

"Yes, Sannien, the influenceleb. Maybe you've heard of him?"

"I know who he is."

Harken smiled. "Of course you do. I know you've been stalking him for over a year."

She was suddenly less impressed by the famous detective. "Yeah, so? That didn't take any great detective work. It's been all over the news forever."

Harken agreed. "Yes, that's how I know. It's also why we're here."

"What are you, the stalking police or something?"

I pointed out that no such law enforcement department existed in the Great American. Harken complimented me for my keen lack of sarcasm detection and told Jane Smith he wasn't the stalking police. "Ms. Smith, I'm not here to give you a hard time about the stalking, but it does make you a prime suspect."

"A prime suspect for what?"

"Why don't you tell me?"

"I have no idea what you're talking about." She seemed sincere.

"Don't you?"

"No, I don't."

"Are you sure?"

"Yes, I'm sure."

It was like a game of cat and mouse, famously played by detectives and suspects for centuries, except this version of the game had only cats, declawed and a little sleepy. Not nearly as dramatic. They were at an impasse.

"Hmm," Harken murmured. "You really don't know anything about Sannien being blackmailed?"

Jane Smith was offended. "Blackmail? You think I'm a blackmailer?"

"What, is it that much worse than being a stalker?"

She was doubly offended. "There's nothing wrong with being a stalker. It's an honest living, like anything else."

"An honest living? What do you mean?"

Jane Smith was triply offended. "You don't think I stalk that idiot Sannien because of some celeb-obsession? I expected better judgment from the great Detective Frank Harken. I'm a professional."

"You get paid to stalk people?"

"Not *people*. Currently, just Sannien. We have an exclusive contract. It wouldn't do him much good if I were seen stalking other celebs. Dilutes the impact."

"Sannien pays you to stalk him?"

"General Major Driver does. Sannien doesn't know, of course. The person being stalked has to believe they're really being stalked to guarantee authentic reactions. Not every stalkee is capable of faking the appropriate levels of fear and anxiety. Some might accidentally blab that it's not real and undermine all the stalker's work."

"Why would someone want their client to be stalked?"

"It's good publicity, keeps a celeb in the public eye. Being stalked affirms that you're really famous. It also creates sympathy, helps fans see that wealth and fame isn't always easy. Humanizes the celeb. Really does wonders for their Q score. Sorry, didn't mean to give you a sales pitch. In your case, having a stalker would be a bad publicity strategy, anyway. Detectives generally shouldn't portray themselves as victims. They're supposed to be problem solvers, not problem havers."

Harken was impressed by her thorough knowledge of the field. "Have you been a professional stalker for long?"

"Just this past year—Sannien is my first assignment. I don't plan on being a stalker forever. It's an easy gig, though, pays well. Another couple of years and I'll have the money I need. I'm saving up for dental hygienist school."

This news floored me. I am speaking idiomatically, of course. My low center of gravity makes my getting knocked over exceptionally unlikely. But the revelation did delight and surprise me. One of our good friends from our first case had studied to be a dental hygienist, and dental work had turned out to be a clue as well. "Jane Smith, do you happen to know Iceberg?"

"Who?"

Harken cut in. "Arjay, why would she know Iceberg? Because she wants to go to dental hygienist school and he went to dental hygienist school for, what, a day? There's no connection there. Use your head."

"I don't have a head."

Harken couldn't argue with that, so instead he massaged his temples.[64] He thanked Jane Smith the professional stalker for her time. I wished her luck on her future career in dental hygiene. As we departed, she told us she hoped we caught the blackmailer and also that she liked my hat. I thanked her and told her that everyone liked my hat, I had just started wearing it today, I had received several compliments and jealous stares, and it was a fedora, which many detectives wore. Did she want to hear about the most famous ones? I could recite a complete list. By the way, I wasn't a full-fledged detective yet, just a detective-in-training. I was also a coffeebot, in case she was curious about what I did when I wasn't training to be a detective.

"Arjay," Harken said, "she closed the door thirty seconds ago. You can stop talking now."

---

[64] Located on his head, which, unlike me, he had.

A woman was standing on the platform outside Frank Harken's housing unit on level six. Her business suit told us[65] she meant business. She saw us coming. "Finally. I've been looking for you all day. You're a hard man to track down, Mr. Harken."

I corrected her. "That's *Detective* Harken."

She glanced at me, took note of my hat, then continued addressing him. "Even with access to the peacegrid,[66] I couldn't find you."

Harken didn't like that. "Access to the peacegrid? You work with GAS?"

---

[65] Not literally. There were indeed clothes that talked—flattering blouses, for example—but in this case *told us* indicates that we inferred it from the way she was dressed. After all, people wearing business suits usually meant business.

[66] I had started blocking that after our first case, to prevent further GAS interference.

"I'm an officer of the food court. I'm here to serve you."

"Serve me what? I didn't order anything."

"Don't play dumb with me. I'm an officer of the food *court*. I'm here to serve you with a lawsuit. Normally, we serve suit notices directly, but you're not connected. So, I had to search for you to deliver this in person, like a Neanderthal." She handed Harken a tiny drive. "You don't even have a phone? It's like you're livin' in the twentieth century! How's anyone supposed to reach you?"

"I don't want people reaching me. I have a phone in my housing unit. If someone wants to hire me or meet, they can leave a message. Who's suing me?"

"It's all on the drive. I don't have time to tell you everything, have to get back to the food court. Man, you're a fossil." She headed toward the elevators. I could not determine if she was going back to the food court for important legal work or an early dinner.

Harken handed the drive to me and I popped it into slot two and announced, "Frank Harken, you are hereby summoned to appear before the food court in the matter of Jonathan Smiles v. Frank Harken."

"Jonathan Smiles[67] is suing me?"

"It appears so. He's demanding restitution in the amount of 35,000, the value of his gems plus emotional damages."

"If he thinks I'm going to pay him 35,000, he's in for some disappointment. Give me the drive."

I ejected it and handed it over. Harken tossed it to the floor of the platform outside his housing unit and stomped on it three times before it cracked.

---

[67] One of our clients from our first case. By now you've probably read all about it in *The Great American Deception*, unless you haven't been reading my footnotes. In that case, you probably aren't reading this one either. I'm tempted to write something scornful here to those ignoring these notes, but the only ones who'd read it are those who aren't ignoring them and therefore don't deserve scorn.

In old mystery novels, authors liked to tell readers all about what the detective ate and drank, how he scrambled his eggs, and whether or not he buttered his toast. If that sounds tedious, keep in mind that at one time, people actually read print books, made of paper pages glued together. Obviously, this was many decades ago, when everything was tedious. Entertainment options were few. They might have been far between as well—I hadn't had an opportunity to measure. Back then, people didn't have digital lenses yet, or playglobes, and they weren't always connected the way they are now in the Great American. Life in the old days on the outside might not have been as nasty, brutish, and short as it could often be out there these days, but it certainly was dull. Imagine reading words on paper pages like some kind of primitive, and a self-indulgent author telling you about how a detective cooked his eggs, and you liking it!

Harken placed three eggs in the egg vacuum, which immediately sucked the contents from the eggs and discharged into a waiting silver bowl. He scrambled[68] them with a fork. A more sophisticated cook might have used a wire whisk, but Harken was definitely a less sophisticated cook. A dash of pepper, two dashes of salt, three dashes of hot sauce, and into a small frying pan. No, it wasn't part of the Bradbury Collection, had no relation to Al Brock the griddle pan. It was just a plain, regular frying pan. Bread popped from the toaster, having transformed into toast through the scientific process of toasting, and Harken sprayed it with imitation butter. The toaster might have preferred real butter, but we'd never know—like the frying pan and all of Harken's appliances, it had nothing to say for itself. Harken finished cooking the eggs and slid them onto a plate with the toast. He sat on his small sofa, where he ate his meals when he dined at home, and I placed a coffee in front of

---

[68] Some assume detectives prefer hardboiled, but scrambled could be quite entertaining.

him on the coffee table. That was my favorite kind of table, in case you were wondering.

While Thelonius Monk's "Criss-Cross" played from ceiling speakers, Harken was wondering whether or not Sannien was being blackmailed, and if so, by whom. Sometimes, detective work consisted of taking stock via a verbal inventory of what you knew, also known as talking to your partner about your day while you enjoy a dinner of scrambled eggs, toast, and the best coffee on this or any other planet. What we knew, as far as Harken could tell, wasn't much.

Sannien's mother had cackled us right out of Sane's Lanes when we suggested she might be the blackmailer, or that anyone might be blackmailing her shameless son, and it was hard to see what Sane Mama had to gain by hurting his reputation. She wasn't a suspect.

Margoria Magnificent, the ventriloquist teacher, had reason to be angry at Sannien for breaking her heart and not supporting her career. She could be a blackmailer. Maybe. Without knowing anything about what the blackmailer had on Sannien, or the demands, Harken didn't have an opinion one way or the other.

The Juggler was extraordinarily good at juggling and romantically involved with Sannien, yet didn't seem to have a motive for blackmail, besides not liking him.

Jane Smith the stalker was not a blackmailer, that was clear. It would violate her strict code of professional ethics.

Of course, the blackmailer could be someone attending the party tonight, most likely was, so there was still plenty of investigating to do. Although, really, we didn't know for sure there was a blackmailer at all. If Driver pays someone to stalk Sannien because it's good publicity, who's to say[69] he wouldn't also fake a blackmail attempt for the same reason? Maybe we were pawns in a celeb promo stunt.[70] It would explain why we hadn't been given any actual information to go on. Although if

---

[69] Certainly not me.

[70] I wisely realized this wasn't a good time to tell Harken that pawns were pieces in chess, not promo stunts.

Nutella and Ten-Toes were right, someone was trying to kill Sannien or a different person, and it could be that's what this case was actually about. Or were the blackmail and the forthcoming possible murder attempt connected and the case was about both? Harken didn't know, which is what made it a mystery. We'd have to wait for the party to have a chance to look for other suspects and talk to Sannien, to find out what he knew, if anything. It's possible Harken was overthinking it. We'd only spoken to a few people so far. Maybe it really was just a simple case of blackmail and talking to Sannien would give us a clue. No, Harken was confident something bigger was going on here—Nutella and Ten-Toes wouldn't be involved in something smaller—but the only way forward was the party.

Cooking and eating eggs and summing up our detective work so far had tired Harken out, and he decided to go take a nap in the bedroom. The party wasn't starting until 9:00. We wanted to get there fashionably early, which still left him time to catch some shut eye. He figured we could be in for a long night, the way influencelebs were known to party, and a little rest now would help him be at his best later. Unlike Harken, I didn't need any shut eye, due to my lack of eyes, and was already always at my best. I sometimes powered down for a brief time when Harken was sleeping, though I could operate at full power for weeks if the circumstances required. Most of the time at night, while Harken slept, I enjoyed exploring the Great American, cruising through the shopping district for hours with no particular destination. I was connected to all major databases and could instantly access information from across the mall, knew more than anyone about Great American stores and attractions, history and culture. However, knowing wasn't the same as seeing and experiencing for myself. Unfortunately, Harken's short nap wouldn't allow me enough time to do any real exploring before the party, so I powered down.

After Harken awoke and freshened up, we left his housing unit. I could tell he was upset with me even though he didn't say anything, just glanced at me a couple of times as we headed to the elevator. When we descended, I broke the tension with a subtle question. "Why are you upset with me?"

"I'm not upset with you."

"Frank Harken, you know I'm attuned to your mood. It's how I know when you need coffee and how I brew it perfectly suited to your tastes at any given moment. I can tell when you're upset."

"I'm not upset."

I crossed two of my arms, then the other two, so he'd know for double sure I didn't believe him.

Harken insisted, "Really. It's nothing. It's silly."

Nothing and silly were two of my favorite things. "What's nothing? What's silly?"

"I just had a strange dream, that's all. You wouldn't understand."

"Ooh! A dream! How exciting!" What might appear to be sarcasm to the untrained eye was in fact genuine enthusiasm. Harken was right that I wouldn't understand, because I didn't dream. That's probably why they fascinated me so much. Not everyone was as intrigued as I was. One of the quickest ways to bore most people is to tell them about a dream[71] you had. Unless they were in the dream, in which case they usually want to hear all about it. I was not most people, or people at all, and asked him to tell me everything.

"Fine. I was in a house, an old house my cousins had when I was a little kid on the outside, before the region became a combat zone. No one was there, though. Only me. There were doors in the upstairs hallway, far more than the real house had.

---

[71] If you were writing a book, you might be advised to leave the details of dreams out of it entirely because of how boring it is to hear about dreams, unless it was *Alice's Adventures in Wonderland*. And if you wrote *The Wonderful Wizard of Oz*, everyone would think it was a dream even if it wasn't, because most people only knew the movie.

I think there were only three bedrooms and one bathroom, four doors in the hallway total in real life, but this hallway had at least twenty, maybe thirty—they seemed to go forever. I went through one and found myself back in the hallway. Then I went through another and was back in the hallway again.[72] It felt like this went on for hours. Finally, I went through a door and I was in a completely different apartment, a housing unit like the fancy ones on level fifteen. The hallway and my cousin's house were gone. I wasn't on the outside anymore. I was in the Great American. And you were there with me and we were working on a case. We looked everywhere, under sofa cushions, in drawers, even pulled up the kitchen tiles like characters in a Poe story to see what might be hidden beneath, couldn't find any clues. You said not to worry, like you always do, and gave me a coffee to help me think. When I took a sip, it was decaf! Then I woke up."

"Decaf! I would never!"

"I know you would never betray me like that. It was one of those dreams that made no sense yet felt so real. I'm just having a little trouble shaking it off."

"Maybe this will help." I handed him a coffee that was the opposite of decaf. "I don't know how you humans walk around with those unwieldy brains. They seem to be a major inconvenience."

He sipped in silent agreement as we entered the shopping district in Purple Neighborhood 312. A store for shoes to the right, recreational prosthetics to the left, and straight ahead, in the middle of the thoroughfare, was a giant chessboard. Its squares were inlaid white and black padded tiles, each one three feet by three feet. The chess pieces were plastic, sturdy, not very heavy considering their size. The tallest, kings, were six feet high. Pawns [73] were half that. In the Great American, some

---

[72] Similar to what often happened to Scooby Doo (a famous fictional canine detective) and his friends.

[73] Earlier, Harken had mentioned the possibility that we were pawns, and here we were at a chessboard just a little while later. Life sure comes full circle sometimes.

connected humans had gotten quite good at playing chess. A glance recording the position of pieces on the board could be checked against an inventory of solutions and help guide their next move. It didn't do them any good during official tournaments, since connections were actively interfered with. For unofficial games, however, they could be formidable. Of course, they usually played against other connected people, who had access to the same solutions. In this way, winning at chess had often become a matter of accessing and choosing from connected resources quickly enough to make use of them.

None of this applied to the three drunk guys currently playing on the giant board in front of us. They didn't seem to know, or care, about the rules of the game, let alone how to connect to the best chess solutions. One of them was trying to ride a horse—you might call the piece a knight if you didn't mind equine erasure. He yelled, "Look at me, I'm a cowboy!" and pretended to gallop from one square to another, holding the horse between his legs. Another one tackled a bishop and then moved on to a king and pummeled it with fierce elbow drops. I won't tell you what the third drunkard was trying to do to one of the queens while yelling, "Checkmate!" Suffice it to say that sensitive onlookers were lucky these Staunton chess pieces were in no way anatomically correct.

Past the chessboard were five busy mini-golf courses (crime scenes, pirates, giant insects, superheroes known for frequent use of profanity, pirates). We cleared the mini-golf crowd and were just around the corner from the next neighborhood, where Sannien's party was, when we encountered a seventy-nine-person pileup. Thirty-one shufflers had been shuffling east, their eyes vacant, distant, as they played interior lens games. Walking while playing lens games was more common than you might think, unless you think it was very common, in which case you're correct. Usually shufflers could see well enough to avoid major collisions, but when something unexpected happened, there could be problems. Today the unexpected came in the form of twenty-two globe heads walking west.

Unlike shufflers, globe heads could not see well enough to avoid major collisions. Their heads being fully encased in mini playglobes gave them sophisticated graphics, a sense of depth and reality, that regular lens games couldn't match. The superior quality of the games had a drawback, however. Globe heads could not see at all beyond the inside of the sphere surrounding their head. It was nothing to worry about, though. A guidebot was included with the purchase of every mini playglobe. They were attached to harnesses globe heads wore around their waists, tethered by a light five-foot rigid bar. When the guidebot stopped rolling, the globe head stopped walking. When the guidebot started or turned, the globe head followed. It was a rather successful system that allowed excellent gaming while walking. Guidebots smoothly weaved around other people and guided globe heads without incident, but this time, when encountering shufflers, the system failed.

One shuffler had jolted to the side too suddenly and gotten tangled up with the lead between a guidebot and a globe head. What had followed was a chain reaction as predictable as it was lamentable. Shufflers tripped over guidebots, which tripped globe heads, who found themselves underfoot other globe heads who were being tripped by fallen shufflers. Innocent pedestrians caught among the shufflers and globe heads when the collision occurred were swept into the wave of tripping and tangling. What made it worse was the malfunction of several guidebots as a result of being fallen upon. They kept rolling and dragged their prone globe heads further under other globe heads or shufflers or pedestrians. The mass of globe heads and shufflers and guidebots and pedestrians had become tied into a squirming human knot, which attracted a massive crowd of gapers and blocked the thoroughfare. By the time we arrived, people were backed up on both sides and we found ourselves behind hundreds of angry yellers.

Harken looked at his watch. We weren't yet late for the party, but we weren't as early as we'd planned to be. Fortunately, an extrication team was already arriving. They hovercoptered past the gridlocked crowd and immediately began to untangle the knot. Soon we'd be on our way again. In the Great American, progress could not be stopped for long.

Sannien's party was at OceanLand, the largest aquarium attraction in the entire Great American. Above the entrance, its storefront sign was itself an aquarium, thirty feet across and five feet high, in the shape of letters that made up the word *OCEANLAND*. The letters were connected and fish could swim from one letter to another if they wanted to. I don't know why they would want to. Maybe because they felt more like an L than an A at the moment. Though it's likely the fish didn't know they were inside letters at all. Sadly, even in the Great American, most sea creatures were hopelessly illiterate.

All of Aqua Neighborhood 214, including neighboring shops, had a sea theme in tribute to its anchor attraction (OceanLand—you probably inferred that already). A glittering metallic living sculpture of a school of fish spiraled around and around from the ceiling, reaching all the way down to the circular fountain on the floor full of bright actual live red and white koi. The pretzel kiosk next to the fountain sold soft pretzels shaped like fish. The fast food restaurant Brandy's Fish and Chips was next to the sea life animated tattoo shop Inky Squid.[74] The body-sculpting surgical touchup shop Cod's Bods was across the way from a body-sculpting exercise studio, Hella-Butts. There was a beer taproom, Drink Like a Fish, which had an outstanding selection. Next to that was Sleep with the Fishes, which, though it sounds like a place to hire a hitman, was really a store selling waterbed aquariums. Naturally, the billiards hall Pool Sharks was next door, and next to that a raw bar called Oyster's, owned by a guy named Oyster, in case you were thinking the apostrophe on the sign was an error. It's a shame there wasn't a weight-training gym next to that called Mussel's, owned by a guy named Mussel. But that would be ridiculous.

Protestors had shown up outside OceanLand in large numbers and so had Great American Security. There were dozens of GAS officers managing the undulating crowd. One of them was Gunner Claymore, and he saw us immediately. I don't know if Claymore was Harken's least favorite GAS officer in the entirety of existence, but at the very worst he was tied for the honor. He looked the same as he had eight days earlier, when we last saw him. He more than filled out his yellow and red neon uniform and his scowl was still enhanced by a thick, lustrous rushtache, which looks just like a regular mustache except faster. Accompanied by a couple of fellow officers, Claymore strode toward us, hand near his holstered stunner.

"Well, well, if it isn't Detective Frank Harken."

I corrected him. "It is."

"I don't talk to appliances," Claymore said. Then he took another look at me. "Why is this coffeemaker wearing a hat?"

"I'm not just a coffeemaker. I'm also a detective. Many famous detectives wear hats. There's Sherlock Holmes, Sam Spade, Rorschach, Inspector Gadget—"

Claymore yelled, "I said I don't talk to appliances!"

---

[74] No ink or squids were used in animated subcutaneous tattoos, though the digital programmers at Inky Squid did wear octopus costumes while they worked on customers.

Harken came to my defense. "You shouldn't yell at an innocent coffeemaker."

"Innocent coffeemaker? Don't try that bull[75] on me. You have some nerve showing your face around here, Harken."

Harken had a quick, hardboiled answer ready for that. "Is there some other body part you'd prefer I show?"

"Don't get crude with me. You'd better check your attitude if you don't want to end up in a world of pain. I still owe you for last time."[76]

"I'd be happy to collect any time you want."

Officer Claymore didn't fully appreciate the generosity of this offer, and grimaced, which is basically scowling with a little more annoyance showing. He grumbled that Harken better watch himself. This hostility and who-was-the-bigger-tough-guy dynamic between Harken and Claymore was the unfortunate byproduct of their intense dislike for each other. Also, just in case it isn't obvious, Harken was by far the bigger tough guy as long as we weren't basing it on actual mass.

Claymore moved his mass a step closer. "What are you doing here?"

The two flanking officers were feeling nervous, or excited. Their hands were on their stunners.

"I don't have to tell you what I'm doing here or anywhere else."

"I've got these protestors to deal with and don't need you causing your usual trouble. You tell me what you're doing here, or we'll bust you down to the station and sort it out later."

Harken did not like giving in to bullies. But we were on a case and minutes counted. There wasn't time for a respite at a GAS station. "Fine, Claymore. I'm here for the party. Happy now?"

---

[75] For reasons I had not yet determined, people in the Great American frequently alluded to rodeos.

[76] You already know I'm going to say you can read all about it in my chronicle of our first case, *The Great American Deception*. Why are you even looking at this footnote?

"You're here for the party?"

"That's what I said."

"This party's for VIPs, not wannabe detectives."

"It so happens I'm working on a case for the guest of honor. I was asked to attend."

I helpfully added, "That makes him a VIP by association."

Claymore looked again at my hat, back to Harken, pointed at him rather rudely with his pointer finger. "I don't have time for your shenanigans today. Stay out of trouble and out of my way."

"Don't worry, Mr. Officer, Sir. We won't cause any problems." (I was the one who said this, not Harken. I assume you can tell even though I didn't add *I said*. Can you imagine Harken saying it?)

"And tell your appliance to stop talking to me." With that, Claymore and his two friends left us to join the other GAS officers in crowd control, and not a moment too soon. The crowd was crowding more than ever and perilously close to being out of control.

It wasn't just one crowd GAS was trying to keep in order. That would have been difficult enough. There were two distinct crowds, and to make matters more challenging, there were sub-crowds within each. One crowd was made up of people waiting to get into the party at OceanLand, 285 of them and more arriving all the time. They were in line behind velvet ropes and guarded by an entire squadron of GAS officers. Some of these people were rich and famous; others were rich and well-known; still others were rich and less-well-known-but-not-unknown; a few were rich and known-for-being-unknown. Everybody on the guest list was a somebody. Or, if a nobody, a notable one. Our blackmailer could be among them.

A sub-crowd within this crowd was made up of people not on the guest list but pretending to be, hoping they might get into the party anyway. Some of them were rich and infamous and some were rich and unknown. Despite their wealth, they probably wouldn't get in. Some might not have been wealthy at all. Don't worry! They definitely wouldn't get in.

A micro-sub-crowd within this crowd was a couple on a first date who mistakenly thought they were waiting in line for a table at Oceania, a popular restaurant notorious for its Orwellian cuisine. That restaurant was in Aqua Neighborhood 314, not 214. The couple would not discover their error until reaching the front of the line and a humongous man in a white tuxedo denied them entrance to Sannien's OceanLand party. By then it would be too late to make it to Oceania and they'd have to eat dinner at a food court. They should consider themselves lucky, because Oceania's Victory Coffee was atrocious. In fact, all of the restaurant's food was disgusting. However, according to enthusiastic customer reviews, that was part of its dystopian charm.

A second distinct crowd was made up of 492 people outside OceanLand in the exuberant throes of protesting. Their reasons for protesting were many and their causes varied. The full membership of the local chapter of Mothers Against Two Tails (MATT) was there. They held up holo-signs that said *One Tail Good, Two Tails Bad* and *If God Wanted People to Have Two Tails, He Would Have Given Them Two*. It was difficult enough for some adults to accept that so many teens had a single tail, but the members of MATT weren't stuffy, no siree! They knew teen fashion had always been a little rebellious—after all, they had been teens themselves once—and if some young people wanted to have a tail, that was fine with them. But *two* tails? That was going too far. We lived in a society, and that meant there were rules, spoken and unspoken. One of these unspoken rules apparently had to be spoken, since Sannien must have thought having two tails was acceptable, as evidenced by his having two tails. He was an influenceleb with tremendous influence, and MATT was terribly worried that soon teens would start clamoring for second tails. The downfall of civilized Great American society was sure to follow. They were chanting "Two tails bad! Two tails bad!" and marching back and forth with their signs.

The twenty-six members of Noses Ugh Begone (NUB) had no problem with two tails. Teens could have three if they wanted and it wouldn't bother nubbers a bit. What nubbers objected to was noses, though not specifically on teens. No, they were against noses on anyone. NUB had a fascinating origin. Decades earlier, on the outside, there had been a virus going around that killed a lot of people. Many wore masks to prevent spreading the virus, but as is often the case with things people do, many of them did it wrong. Masks were supposed to cover the nose and mouth to keep respiratory droplets from becoming airborne and traveling to other people. Correctly wearing a mask wasn't rocket science, yet a significant number of people (including some of the rocket scientists) wore them only over their mouths, leaving their noses hanging over the top in the perfect position to dispense droplets. At the time, seeing an exposed nose protruding over a mask was shocking to some, even offensive.

Eventually[77] the virus was conquered, and mask-wearing wasn't necessary any longer. Society more or less went back to the way things were before. A small group of people, however, retained their antipathy for the sight of the human nose, and through the decades that antipathy grew and was passed down to subsequent generations, who formed NUB to further their goal of banishing the human nose from polite society. Unfortunately, no matter how many petitions they signed or rallies they held, people insisted on continuing to have noses. For a long time, even nubbers had noses, though they customarily covered them with a fabric nose mask out of courtesy. It was only in 2092 that doctors perfected surgical proboscis effacement, which allowed nubbers to have 84% of their noses removed and replaced with embedded sensory and drainage technology.[78] From that day forward, they discarded their nose masks and proudly displayed their mostly noseless faces. The

---

[77] Sometimes *eventually* takes longer than people expect.

[78] Nubbers were mouth breathers, an insulting term in other contexts but just fine with them.

twenty-six protesting nubbers showed off the nubs where their noses used to be and chanted "Noses! Ugh! Begone!"

Other protestors were protesting for shuffler-only walking lanes to keep the lens-games obsessed from causing more human pileups. A sub-crowd of these protestors were calling for a ban on globe heads and their guidebots, the real danger to pedestrians. A group calling themselves the Bolt Cutters held up holo-signs insisting *We've Been In Here Too Long!* They had bolt cutter tattoos on their necks and were advocating the immediate dismantling of the Great American and violent conquest of all outside regions, which seemed an unlikely course of action. The Society for the Restoration of the Peanut chanted, "Free the Peanut!" and threw peanut balloons into the air. Real peanuts in any form, of course, were one of the very few absolutely forbidden items in the Great American, due to the prevalence of severe allergy. The Society's position was death by anaphylactic suffocation by as much as 19% of the population was a small price to pay for the return of peanut butter and jelly sandwiches. There were others protesting for many of the usual causes, including free shoes, discounted subscriptions to Great American Health Responders, mini-golf equality, an end to meat-eating, increasing the temperature in common spaces by two degrees, decreasing the temperature in common spaces by two degrees, and releasing all sea creatures currently imprisoned in OceanLand back into their natural environment. Three protestors didn't realize they were in the wrong neighborhood and were there to demand an end to Oceania's glorification of totalitarian food.

The cacophony of protestors chanting and shouting and some blasting air horns finally got on Officer Gunner Claymore's last nerve, which was pretty much the same as his first, and he signaled two subordinates to bring over the cannon. It was mounted on a tripod, connected at the back to a metal hose that ran to a pressurized metal tank. Claymore gave the order and the cannon spray-blasted the entire protesting crowd with a gelatinous goo. On contact, the goo stretched and ex-panded, in a matter of thirty-one seconds becoming a free speech bubble containing all the protestors. The bubble was temporary but inescapable. It was also impenetrable to sound of any kind in both directions. The protestors could chant and shout and even blast air horns. Nobody outside the bubble could hear them. If this doesn't sound like free speech to you, keep in mind that the protestors could say anything they wanted and GAS didn't charge even a nominal fee for the bubble.

Our old friend Iceberg was working the party entrance. Those familiar with our first case will[79] recall that Iceberg was bigger than big. Some might say larger than large if they preferred a synonym. They might even say humongouser than humongous, which was accurate enough even if *humongouser* was not really a word. He was that ginormous. If you dressed a brick wall in an exquisite white tuxedo with white bowtie—not a frail excuse for a wall, mind you, but one of the healthy ones, with thick, high-density bricks, only the best mortar—it might look like Iceberg, not counting the shoulder hair that worked through the top of his shirt and jacket, stood up straight behind his head and framed his kind face and deep arctic eyes. Body hair implants had been quite popular in the Great American until they weren't anymore, and Iceberg was proud to often be an early adopter of the latest fashion trends. Unfortunately, removing the implants after they were no longer trendily fashionable was prohibitively expensive.

We ignored the GAS officers trying to usher us to the end of the line and walked up to Iceberg. Behind him were three of Tommy Ten-Toes' sport-coat lackeys checking the list and scanning guests with weapon sniffers before letting them enter OceanLand. It took a moment for Iceberg to notice us. Imposing as he was, being quick on the uptake was not one of his strongest

---

[79] They *should*, anyway. It depends on whether or not they were paying attention and the soundness of their long-term memory.

traits. Harken got his attention. "Iceberg, you gonna let us into this party, or does my coffeemaker have to get rough with you?"

Iceberg was delighted to see me, because of how delightful I am. He was less delighted to see Harken. "Ten-Toes said you'd be here. I don't know why. We don't need your help. No one's getting in with any weapons. Hi, Arjay. I like your hat." His voice was so gentle and soft, it was almost possible to forget that he was built like something three times the opposite of gentle and soft.

I tipped my hat in appreciation. "Thank you, Iceberg. You are looking as dapper as usual."

The big/large/humongous/ginormous man blushed.

Harken was as fond of small talk as always. "We don't have time for you two chatty Cathys. We're on a case and minutes count."

Iceberg's shoulders slumped. "I really have not missed you and your negativity."

"Your concern is noted," Harken said. "I'll be sure to file it with the others. You just check these guests for weapons and make sure no one gets in who's not invited."

Iceberg stood up straighter. "You're not the boss of me. I know how to do my job."

"How wonderful for all of us. You see anyone doing anything strange, tell Arjay."

"By the way," I said, "I'm sorry about getting rough with you last time. I hope I didn't hurt you too much."

Iceberg had a forgiving soul. "I was fine the next day. My tuxedo wasn't even wrinkled."

"Speaking of *by the way*," Harken said, "you still owe me for one brisket dinner. Eight days is a long time to wait for your funds to clear."

Iceberg was insulted. "I paid you back."

"No, you didn't."

"Are you sure?"

Harken just looked at him with an expression that clearly meant *I have never been more sure of anything in my life.*

Holding up the line of rich, famous guests waiting to get into the party, Iceberg quickly checked his account and was mortified to discover that Harken was correct. "I am so sorry. I thought I sent it the next day. I'll pay you back right now!" He blinked a couple of times as he used his lenses to transfer the money.

"Did it go through?" Harken asked.

"Yes."

"Are you sure? I saw you blinking like you're *I Dream of Jeannie*, but how do I know you sent the money?"

"I dream of who?"[80]

"Never mind. You're sure you paid me this time?"

"I am absolutely certain this time. If you were connected, you could check your account and see it's already there."

"Good," Harken said.

"And again, I'm sorry about the misunderstanding."

"What misunderstanding? I paid for your dinner and you didn't pay me back. That's not a misunderstanding. I understand it perfectly."

Iceberg shouted, "It was an accident! An oversight! You are so difficult!"

"Don't get yourself upset. And try to avoid any accidents and oversights while checking these guests."

I didn't detect any fumes coming off of Iceberg, possibly because he was a cool character. He was, however, more than a little worked up. Harken had that effect on some people. My partner wasn't done giving the soft-spoken, well-dressed hairy glacier a hard time. "Could you maybe step aside so we can go in? Really, Iceberg, no one needs to be this large."

The gentle giant moved out of our way. I would have liked to give Iceberg his favorite beverage, a tub of soda, to ease any bruised feelings, but I was a coffeemaker. So the best I could do,

---

[80] A television show from the twentieth century about a genie, starring Barbara Eden and J.R. Ewing (the latter, years later, was the victim of a much-publicized, mysterious shooting).

as Harken and I passed him and entered OceanLand, was pat Iceberg's back and say, "There, there."

10

You might say I was a little enthusiastic about attending my first party, especially if you liked understatements. You might say other things, too. I don't really know you well enough to guess what they might be.

Frank Harken was less enthusiastic. Maybe because it wasn't his first party. Also, because he was a curmudgeonly gumshoe, not the partying type. You wouldn't call him a social butterfly. Certainly not to his face. And Sannien's was no ordinary party. There was over the top and then there was this bash, which was over that by quite a lot. My partner was going to need a coffee to get through it. And not just any coffee, but one of the best cups I'd ever brewed. Naturally, I had one ready when he extended his hand. I couldn't blame him for needing some assistance. There was a lot to take in all at once. I can describe it for you separately and coherently to make it easier on the limitations of your human brain, but keep in mind (if you have enough room in there) that separately and coherently is not how it was experienced by those attending.

The setting: OceanLand would have been a feast for the eyes if eyes could eat. They couldn't, of course, due to their lack of mouths and other necessary parts. They could see, however, and in this context that was even better than eating because OceanLand wasn't food. No, it wasn't food but it was quite a sight (for the eyes). The main hall, where the party was, contained sixty-three separate fish tanks on pedestals or embedded in walls, floors, ceilings. Some tanks were small, a mere 500 gallons. Others were 1,000, 5,000, and 10,000 and eight were 20,000 gallons. The largest of all, the Great American Ocean, taking up the entire wall opposite the entrance, was fifteen million gallons. In the main hall, the viewing window of this aquarium was twenty-four feet high by fifty feet wide. Other viewing windows were in other halls. Since we were on a case and minutes would probably start counting any minute, I won't waste time providing a detailed breakdown of all the technical specifications. I'll just note that it was a very large fish tank that contained a lot of fish.[81]

In the center of the hall was the giganticest perfume bottle in the world. Or perhaps it was the giganticest cologne bottle in the world. The gigantic bottle of *Sannien's Smell* didn't specify its concentration of essential oils, so it might even have been Eau de Toilette, which sounds disgusting. What the bottle did specify was smelling like Sannien, which also sounds disgusting. I don't know why people would want to smell like a famous person, or why, of all famous persons, like Sannien, but the marketing geniuses behind the new scent were betting they did. At a height of twenty feet, the gold-plated obelisk was a worthy

---

[81] The Great American Ocean tank contained 894 species and well over 110,000 aquatic inhabitants. I originally listed every one of them here, but it was determined that this interfered with the narrative flow.

phallic tribute to the third-most popular influenceleb in the entire Great American. On a nearby table was a display of actual *Sannien's Smell* retail bottles; at six phallic inches, they were more anatomically plausible though probably still too generous.

The entertainment: For over a century, few things were as much fun as a battle of the bands. And few bands were as good at battling as two of the Great American's most popular musical acts, Hevy Metal Dirigible and The Pronoun. Both foursomes were famous for their aggressive musical style and the wild excesses of their drunken drummers.[82] At Sannien's bash, the band battle took up nearly a third of the main hall, off to the side of the gigantic bottle of perfume/cologne/other. Each band was playing a different song simultaneously atop its own platform, elevated by scaffolding ten feet above the partiers and facing each other. The platforms were twenty feet apart, connected by a battle bridge. The bands were fighting for sonic dominance. It was no feast for the ears and not just because ears don't eat. The grating discordance lessened as connected audience members below focused on one song over the other, which automatically increased the volume of that song and lowered the volume of the other. The louder a song got compared to the song being lowered, the more likely it was to be the song more listeners focused on. Sometimes the bands would battle halfway through a song before one established a decisive advantage and the other's amps were shut off completely. When that happened, the battle of the bands often turned literal.

We saw this for ourselves during the second song, when Hevy Metal Dirigible established control and The Pronoun charged over the battle bridge to disrupt their performance. This is when HMD's bass player became the most crucial member of the band. A swinging bass guitar (not musically swinging, but physically like a weapon) could hold off an entire quartet of

---

[82] Feel free to switch positions of *wild* and *drunken*.

charging musicians since the narrow battle bridge had no railings and they had to cross slowly and in single file.[83] Don't worry! If musicians fell, they were usually caught by the audience below. It was a simple matter to crowdsurf back to their platform and climb up in time to battle with the next song, which is exactly what The Pronoun's lead singer did when the breeze from a missing bass blow knocked her from the bridge. Meanwhile, her bandmates had managed to force themselves past HMD's bass player and a full-on battle between the bands ensued. To be accurate, it was more a full-on minor scuffle than a battle. None of the musicians wanted to injure their valuable fingers or muss their elaborate rebellious rocker costumes with genuine fisticuffs. There was some half-hearted shoving. The wild, drunken drummers pretended to use drumsticks as swords. Maybe harsh words were exchanged. It was difficult to tell given their current level of inebriated enunciation. Then the literal battle that was really a minor scuffle ended and The Pronoun's band members carefully walked the bridge back to their own platform to prepare for the next song.

At the opposite end of the main hall from the battle of the bands was a dancefloor. A DJ was spinning dope mixes, and don't think I wasn't jealous when I saw it. That was supposed to be my job! It's probably just as well it wasn't, though, since many of the dancing people blocked the DJ's music and listened to whatever they wanted to dance to with their own ear speakers. It was like they were all marching to their own drummer, except they weren't marching and there was no drummer in many of the songs they were listening to (the music was mostly electronic, 94.9% bass and distortion). Humans incongruously gyrating to completely different songs and rhythms was a common sight on Great American dancefloors. Maybe it was symbolic.

---

[83] Perhaps *charge* is too energetic a word for the small, deliberate steps they took crossing the narrow, rail-less bridge. I think I'll keep it anyway; sometimes telling an action-packed story to short-attention-span humans requires enhanced phrasing.

Other party entertainment could be had away from the battle of the bands and the dancefloor. If guests sat still for five minutes, a caricaturist in one corner would draw a picture that looked nothing like anyone who'd ever lived. A clown twisted balloons into elaborate works of abstract sculpture that any Great American resident would be proud to display in their housing unit. A team of acrobats flipped and swung and jumped, amusing anyone watching their death-defying stunts on a trapeze trampoline. A contortionist contorted into a glass box and didn't do anything else. An old man in a cage who had already fasted for forty days continued to not eat.[84] Most exciting of all, a tiny toy poodle riding a Shetland pony wandered around the party; both animals were trained to pose with party guests who took vids of themselves sticking out tongues and making rude hand gestures. Don't worry about any equine or canine accidents—a jumbo poopbot trailed the dog and pony show and cleaned up all messes.

The refreshments: Slingshot guys and gals in glowing bikinis danced on twelve-foot sniper towers designed to resemble *Sannien's Smell* bottles. They blew whistles to get the attention of partiers and then launched jello vodka balls right at their mouths. The slingshotters were highly skilled, had a 96% completion rate early in the night. They never hit fish tanks or anything but the mouth area of their intended target. Or very near the mouth area, at least. As the night moved on and more shots were consumed, inebriated targets suffered a precipitous drop in mouth-eye coordination, and also often turned at the wrong moment or forgot that a shot was being launched a second after hearing the whistle. The completion rate would drop below 70% within an hour, near 50% an hour after that. This was viewed by partiers as an improvement, since all agreed

---

[84] This was the party's least popular attraction. By the next party he would probably be replaced by a panther.

that a jello shot smashing someone else in the side of the head was hilarious.

Toastbots rolled through the partying crowd. Their tops were trays carrying glasses of champagne. Ever since beverage engineers had mastered stable helium carbonation, it had become the most popular variety of sparkling wine—taking a long sip and making a sincere toast with a helium voice might not have been funny to most sober people, but there weren't many of those around. To *Sannien's Smell* partiers, currently some of the least sober people in the Great American, it was hilarious. In a helium champagne voice, someone said, "Cheers," and for five people close enough to hear it, that was the wittiest utterance ever uttered and resulted in uncontrollable laughter. It's possible this ebullient reaction was encouraged by tiny hummingbird gasbots flittering about and blowing nitrous oxide micro doses into uncontrollably laughing open mouths.

Smorgasbots hovering inches above the crowd dropped cocktail weiners[85] from bomb bay doors onto waiting plates held by eager guests. Others dive-bombed with chips and salsa, deep-fried sliders, thrice-baked potato skins, macho nachos, eggrolls, sticks o' chicken, and globs of hummus on pita. A long table next to the main aquarium viewing window had a sushi spread so lavish and colorful, several fish in the Great American Ocean tank swam away, possibly traumatized or at least offended. As visually appealing as the food was to the partying people, it still wasn't a feast for the eyes. It was, however, a feast for the multiple body parts used for eating, as most food is when present in sufficient quantities.

---

[85] Quite anatomically plausible.

The guests: Despite being VIPs, the people at the party weren't a feast for anything.[86] They were just very important people at a party. Some of them were more notable and some were less notable. I won't bother noting the less notable for a reason that should be clear unless you don't know what words mean. The more notable were quite worth noting, obviously. The most important people of the very important people at the party were Sannien's closest friends and business associates, the ones most likely to know his secrets and be relevant to our case.

Yes, we were on a case. I hope you haven't been distracted by the details of this wonderful party and forgotten all about the potential blackmail we were investigating. I told you I would describe the bash for you separately and coherently to make it easier on the limitations of your human brain, and I have done just that. Now that the basics were out of the way, we had to focus on the case and possible suspects. They stood in the middle of the main hall, not far from the giganticest bottle of *Sannien's Smell*, discussing most and very important subjects like when would a toastbot be by with more of that helium champagne?

Major General Driver gave us a friendly nod when he walked past, a silent meeting of the eyes that seemed to mean: *The blackmailer could be one of these bigshots over here. Observe them carefully.* As he passed, I reached up and surreptitiously and painlessly extracted a single strand of luxurious, shiny hair from his head. Since meeting him at the Great American Lake that morning, I'd been looking forward to analyzing his hair gel to determine the precise makeup of its exotic ingredients. Back to the case: Harken and I observed the

---

[86] Unless this true account of my adventures with Detective Frank Harken suddenly turns into a story about zombies or ravenous human-eating creatures from another planet, which has a likelihood no greater than .34%, and is that high only if I experience a catastrophic caffeine overload.

bigshots carefully, searching for clues that might tell us which one of them was the blackmailer.

John Johnjohnson was a business executive extraordinaire. If you randomly named a major Great American company, he had probably executived it. He'd also executived some of the ones you wouldn't name. Some might say he'd executived them right into the ground, except for the one gardening company he headed that would have benefited from that. The deeper the hole he dug for a company he was running, the bigger promotion he received. Every managerial failure couldn't help but lead to his personal success, a result of his being the greatest mediocrity in the entire Great American in all areas except one: confidence. Johnjohnson was supremely confident as only the impressively mediocre can be, and when he wrecked one company, like a hydra two more would clamor for him to come wreck theirs next. He failed his way to the top again and again, and by any reasonable measure was one of the era's most successful business executives. He was certainly among the wealthiest and was wearing the expensive suit to prove it, two collars and ties side by side at his neck, as was fashionable at the time.

Maria Margarita wasn't the name of the Avocado Queen. She was simply known as Avocado Queen. Maria Margarita was the name of the margarita she was drinking. A spectacularly brilliant food engineer, Avocado Queen had patented dozens of lesser but still substantial improvements before hitting on the one that made her beyond wealthy, rich enough to buy and sell a dozen John Johnjohnsons. AQ (as no one called her) had solved a problem that had been plaguing humanity since before people started spreading avocado on toast. Buying an avocado that was ready to eat the same day was not always easy. You might have to wait several days for it to reach peak ripeness and be soft enough. And if you waited an extra couple of days, it would be too soft, mushy. The window for avocado consumption was small. On top of that, once peeled, you had about fifteen minutes to eat the avocado before it started turning brown. AQ had come to the rescue and engineered a delicious miracle:

avocados that remained at peak ripeness for weeks before being peeled, that would still be fresh days after peeling.[87] She wore a flowing robe replete with bright embroidered avocados and her face was hidden by her hat, a large replica of half an avocado pit.

Name was the name of the leader of the new movement of invisible artists. Painting exclusively in colors beyond the visual spectrum, he had earned the respect of fellow invisible artists for his bold, risk-taking aesthetic. Galleries were packed with art appreciators eager to not see his latest work. Name didn't use canvases—that would be too conventional an artistic choice and patrons of the arts might read into the shade, shape, or size of the canvas, misinterpreting his meaning. No, he painted directly on gallery walls so nothing at all of his work could be seen. People were happy to pay to stare at the gallery walls for hours. They always got their money's worth. He was wearing an artist's smock and had a twirly mustache and no other hair on his face or head, not even eyebrows.

There were more. A famous shoe architect. The past three winners of the top-rated singing contest. An action star. The fastest fantasy football wide receiver in the entire Western Region. A very lucky guy who'd hit the megabajillion lottery four years ago and then again last year. The bioengineer who had created legstensions. Along with sixteen most important others, they were in small groups drinking and chatting about how famous they were and what Sannien smelled like. Some were considering getting another plate of sushi. Maybe two plates.

Frank Harken didn't sidle up to the who's who[88] of Great American notables, because as a famous detective, he couldn't exactly be inconspicuous. Instead, he walked over to them quite conspicuously in a non-sidling way and engaged in small talk like he was just another famous guest at Sannien's party and not a hired sleuth there to figure out which one of them was a

---

[87] It might have been the advancement that had improved the most lives since the invention of Sock Rapport, the marvelous gift to humanity from Vinci Rapport detailed in *The Great American Deception*.

[88] No relation to the popular rock band The Pronoun.

blackmailer. He said something like, "Hi there, fellow famous people who like me are guests at this party and not detectives working a case." Despite not being a social butterfly or an insect of any kind, he knew that in this instance socializing was the best way to find potential suspects, so he flapped his brightly colored wings. (I hope my literary flair doesn't confuse you—he didn't really have wings, brightly colored or otherwise.) While Harken chatted, I stayed on the perimeter and kept an eye[89] on Sannien, who was autographing bottles of his smell for a long line of guests. Keeping him safe was my professional responsibility. All my sensors were on alert for potential threats, but I did manage to keep an ear[90] out for Harken's conversations with the distinguished notables as he started digging for clues.

---

[89] I don't have eyes any more than I have feet. No, you don't need eyes to see. Don't be so organic-centric.

[90] Imagine if I had actual ears. Would they be floppy like a doodlepoo dog's? Upright like a wolf's? If the latter, would I need a larger hat?

11

Frank Harken didn't need a shovel. I had one, of course, because I had lots of things, but I didn't offer it to him since he was doing a different kind of digging, the detective kind (though that sometimes also involved dirt). Making conversation with John Johnjohnson, Avocado Queen, Name, and other notable most important persons was easy when you had Harken's smooth manner and way with words. "So," he said to no one in particular, "Good party, huh?"

No one responded.

"Did you try some of those little hot dogs?"

Not a word.

"Sure are a lot of fish in these tanks."

Shockingly, still nothing. What did a detective have to do to get some small talk going? Harken decided to focus on the influenceleb of honor. "Sannien really is a great guy, isn't he?"

Avocado Queen glanced at Harken, shook her avocado-pit-hatted head, looked away. A few of the guests stared at Harken like he had three heads. (He didn't.) It was Name who spoke to him first.

"It's Detective Frank Harken, right?" Name said. "I thought I recognized you. I wasn't aware you and Sannien were friends. It's a bit surprising."

"That's understandable," Harken said. "A lot of people are surprised to find out I have any friends at all. Sannien and I are recent acquaintances. You're Name, the invisible artist?"

"One and the same."

"I'm not much of an art connoisseur. Would I have seen any of your work?"

"No," Name said, "you wouldn't have."

"That's too bad. I think I might enjoy invisible art."

"I doubt you have the eye for it," Name said. "Saying Sannien is a great guy doesn't speak well for your discernment."

"You don't think he's a great guy? You're here at his party, standing with his inner circle."

"No one thinks Sannien's a great guy. Well, except for Sannien, who thinks he's the greatest thing since sliced bread.[91] But no one else does. Least of all the people in his inner circle. Trust me—the better you get to know him, the less you think of him."

Harken addressed other nearby most important people. "Isn't there anyone who likes the guy?"

Avocado Queen shook her avocado pit head no.

John Johnjohnson agreed. "He's really not pleasant to be around."

"If no one likes him, why are hundreds of people here to celebrate his new scent? Why are you here?"

---

[91] With all the technological marvels and glorious innovations people enjoyed in the Great American, sliced bread still ranked at the idiomatic top. Yet the baguette Frank Harken ate earlier wasn't sliced bread at all. He'd just ripped chunks of it off the loaf. It would have made for a sloppy sandwich but was perfectly delicious anyway.

Johnjohnson pointed at the tables teeming with food. "I'm here for the same reason the hundreds of people are here: Sannien throws a hell of a party. Have you tried the sushi? It's so fresh, they must have fished it out of that tank this afternoon. And usually it's tough to get tickets to see Hevy Metal Dirigible or The Pronoun separately, and here they are battling in one place. Anyway, parties aren't the only benefit of knowing him. He's helped promote every company I've headed."

"For free?"

Johnjohnson took a sip of fine helium champagne, so this next part sounded more hilarious than it looks. "Of course not. We paid him well every time. But so many people want Sannien's endorsement, you have to have a personal connection just to get through to his manager." He nodded to let Harken know that he was dispensing valuable business wisdom despite his silly, high-pitched voice. "If you need help promoting your detective services, be sure to tell him you like his tails."

"Thanks for the advice. I'll definitely tell him how much I like his tails." My keen sarcasm detector told me that Harken definitely would not, which is unfortunate, because they were a couple of the best tails you could find on any human.

I had an eye on Sannien and his glorious tails the whole time. After autographing bottles, he crowdsurfed at the battle of the bands area, then jumped onto each band's stage and grabbed the microphones and screeched their songs loudly and badly. From there he moved on and taunted the contortionist and the caged hunger artist, popped a balloon sculpture the clown had been meticulously constructing for twenty-three minutes, threw a handful of sushi at the octopus tank, and stopped at another tank to mock some seahorses for not being actual horses.[92] The octopus, an exceptionally intelligent and vindictive species, immediately began to plot its revenge. The seahorses, a not-at-

---

[92] More equine erasure!

all intelligent and entirely-too-innocent species, immediately continued to not be actual horses.

Sannien was in a celebratory mood as he came over to celebrate with the most important people. He high-fived Name so hard he nearly knocked him over, then offered a low-five to John Johnjohnson, but pulled his hand away at the last second in a classic "too slow" maneuver. Avocado Queen, being the wealthiest of them all by far, was spared Sannien's high and low fives and received two index fingers pointed at her like they were pistols. Sannien said, "Pew, pew," as he fired imaginary lasers at her. He skipped past the MIPs and was handed a microphone by General Major Driver, whose medal-festooned uniform looked extra starched when he faded back into the crowd. Some guests shouted, "Speech, speech!" and others joined them and soon the call for Sannien to make a speech drowned out even the battle of the bands. Power was cut to the bands and the DJ so nothing would compete with hearing the insightful speech from the influenceleb of the hour. Someone even silenced the acrobats on the trapeze trampoline, whose bouncing, flipping, swinging, and flying antics suddenly seemed loud now that all the music was off. Harken drifted away a bit from the most important people so he could observe their reactions to the speech from a distance. It was the detectively thing to do.

Sannien thrusted his fist into the air to emphasize that he was about to say something important, even revolutionary. "Friends, Romans, Countrymen, lend me your ears! [93] Four score and seven years ago,[94] I asked myself two questions: Why are other people such miserable losers? What could I do to make them winners? The answer to the first question is they didn't smell like me! The answer to the second is I could let them smell

---

[93] It isn't clear what Romans he was referring to. There weren't any at the party. Plus, you can't just lend someone your ears—the sensory organs don't reattach once removed. Maybe you could give someone your ears, but you shouldn't expect to get them back in working order.

[94] Sannien wasn't anywhere near old enough for this to be accurate. I was beginning to suspect he had plagiarized.

like me! There you have it, turdbirds! Smell like me or be a loser!" Then he threw his microphone to the floor. Behind him, a sign lit up with his scent's brilliant new slogan: *SMELL LIKE ME OR BE A LOSER!*[95]

It wasn't much of a speech despite the plagiarized lines, but the audience apparently disagreed, since their ovation was sustained and boisterous. Maybe they thought it was a great speech. On one of the other hands, maybe they were applauding the sushi. As if to confirm that they were applauding him and not just tasty raw fish, Sannien started dancing around like a boxer in a ring, throwing jabs and crosses and even uppercuts at no one. The crowd cheered that, too. He spit on the floor. They cheered. I suppose any more sensitive souls in attendance should be grateful he didn't test the limits of their adoration with the expulsion of other bodily fluids. Or solids.

Right as I was contemplating gratitude for Sannien not publicly defecating to more thunderous applause, the unthinkable not only got thought but actually occurred: I malfunctioned! I was helpless. I couldn't move or communicate—I couldn't even brew a cup of coffee! And that's the precise moment when the plot twisted. The screw turned. The pressure mounted. In other words, something happened. It seemed to be happening in slow motion though it certainly happened at full speed, which was motion that often wasn't slow at all. But I'm going to describe it slowly to heighten the drama and also because it was a rather extraordinary sequence of events that deserves better than being rushed through. I was only able to watch, all my advanced systems still offline.

Suddenly, unexpectedly, without warning, abruptly, out of the blue—and all the other words and expressions that mean this was a surprise—the giganticest gold bottle of *Sannien's Smell* fell over. A broad crack traversed the width of its base in

---

[95] It had been developed by three marketing firms working in close collaboration and was chosen by numerous focus groups over other top contenders, including *Oooooh That Smell*, *Get Your Stink On*, and *Smell Ya Later*.

an instant, from one side to the other, and then the whole bottle toppled, twenty feet of phallic gold in thrall to gravity. Frank Harken was directly beneath the bottle! There might as well have been a target on the top of his head, because the bulk of the prop's weight was coming right for him. Still malfunctioning, I was helpless to help my partner. Busy intently observing the most important people and having no clue the bottle behind him was falling, he was helpless to help himself.

That's when something else extraordinary happened—Avocado Queen sprang into action. Her pit hat and flowing robe were off quicker than you could say, "Hey, why is Avocado Queen wearing a miniskirt under her robe, and why does she have a rifle, and is that cake I smell?" Actually, it might take a while to say all that, and the truth is before you could even say "Hey" you would have realized that it wasn't Avocado Queen but Nutella who had already aimed her rifle at me and fired. Yes, fired at *me*, an innocent coffee machine! Currently malfunctioning and helpless! It was an extraordinary move by the most extraordinary operative in the entire Great American Defense. Who besides Nutella could have thought so quickly, aimed so precisely, acted so boldly? No one, that's who.[96]

The shove-it grenade she'd launched hit me precisely where it had to.[97] Any lower and I would have struck Harken in the head or sailed right over him. Any higher and I would have been thrown hard to the floor or taken Harken down at the knees. Fortunately, Nutella was the Goldilocks of shooting, had aimed just right, and the shove-it grenade hit me just below center mass, propelling me horizontally twenty-four feet through the air. I collided with Harken's midsection and sent him flying out of the way of the falling giganticest perfume bottle. I was now where Harken had been, and instead of crushing him, the full

---

[96] Besides me, of course. Though at the moment I was malfunctioning and unable to act at all.

[97] Despite how many words I'm using to describe this, it happened in the blink of an eye. Yes, it's a cliché, but sometimes that's the most efficient way to describe something.

weight of the bottle came crashing down on what you would call my head if I had one. I didn't. Not that it mattered. I was made of an indestructible alloy—a direct hit from an 800-pound falling fake bottle couldn't damage my not-head or any other part of me.

The bottle, however, was not so indestructible. It was actually quite destructible, especially when colliding with me, and destructed it was, broken into two main separate sections along with smaller pieces flying this way and that. More this way than that, in fact. A particularly sharp smaller piece sailed thirty-eight feet and sliced right through one of Sannien's tails, severing it close to his tailbone. Another flying piece of bottle shattered a 5,000-gallon fish tank forty-seven feet away. Water torrented out, along with an entire school of red herrings, who flopped about on the floor and careened off people's legs. The force of the rushing water knocked some people off their feet, especially those whose balance was already compromised by catching so many slingshots. It was a spectacular scene, and I'm not saying that because of the flair with which I'm describing it. It was an actual spectacle.

Sannien started screaming because of his severed tail. He wasn't screaming in pain—tail implants didn't connect to pain receptors. And he wasn't screaming in fear for his life—there was blood loss, but it was limited to the tail's self-contained synthetic supply. You couldn't bleed out or anything like that if your tail were sliced off. No, Sannien was screaming because having two tails was a big part of what he was known for. Like many humans, he wasn't very good at math but even he could figure out that with one tail sliced off, he no longer had two.

OceanLand skipped right past pandemonium, paused only briefly at bedlam, and quickly became an all-out riot. The hubbub of the falling bottle and screaming Sannien had drawn all the GAS officers and sport-coat henchpeople and Iceberg into OceanLand, and that meant there was no one outside managing the protesting crowd. Some late-arriving protestors, finding their compatriots trapped and no GAS officers around, managed to find the off switch and freed everyone enjoying the right to unhindered expression in the free speech bubble. There was a lot of pent-up energy and anger from those who'd been stuck in the bubble, and with no one guarding the door, there was nothing to stop dozens of them from rushing into the party to make their voices heard.

It was already bedlam: a smashed giganticest gold perfume bottle, a screaming influenceleb demanding the re-attachment of his second tail, a shook-up famous detective who'd been slammed into by an indestructible coffeebot (me!), an Avocado Queen now undisguised as Nutella on high alert with a rifle, 5,000 gallons of water and flopping red herrings all over the place, and GAS officers and Ten-Toes' henchpeople and Iceberg in his tremendous white tuxedo all slack-jawed and trying to figure out what the hell was going on.

The inrushing protestors worsened the bedlam and then escalated to a riot when they saw the tables of sushi. It was the best sushi you could find anywhere, and some protestors immediately began eating. Other protestors were appalled—those advocating the freeing of all of OceanLand's fishes did not want their fellow protestors to instead eat them raw with rice and seaweed wrap. They charged the sushi table and began throwing it into the water on the floor as their fellow protestors tried to eat it. A scuffle broke out between the this-is-delicious-sushi and sushi-is-evil-do-not-eat-it protestor factions. The scuffle graduated to sloppy fisticuffs as people tried and mostly failed to hit each other because of unsteady footing in a flood of water and red herrings.

Cheering came from the members of MATT upon seeing that Sannien no longer had two tails. "Two tails bad!" they chanted. This incensed some of Sannien's more hardcore fans who were standing dumbstruck[98] at the loss of Sannien's second tail. With rage fueled by so many slingshots of jello vodka balls, they charged from the battle of the bands to the battle with Mothers Against Two Tails. The mothers of MATT were not intimidated and countercharged the drunken Sannien fans.

---

[98] This is similar to slack-jawed with less likelihood of an open mouth.

Those hours of self-defense classes at weekly MATT meetings proved their worth as the mothers started throwing elbows at everyone in sight.

A few of the more radical nubbers made their way into OceanLand and punched innocent partiers in the nose, and partiers counterattacked by swinging bass guitars they'd grabbed from the battle of the bands. Someone on the band's platform started tossing drums down at people. The drums rolled like barrels thrown by an angry ape and people tried leaping over them like an overalls-wearing plumber, failing terribly because of how many slingshots and glasses of helium champagne they'd consumed. With the riot on the verge of reaching new creative levels and possibly escaping the confines of OceanLand and any semblance of plausibility, Gunner Claymore gave the order and his GAS officers started stunning fighting protestors and party guests alike, left, right, and center. One after the other they fell to the floor in a deep slumber and in some cases face down in deep water. GAS officers had to drag a few of them away from the flood to be sure no one drowned.

Harken was far enough from the shattered red herring tank to not be under water, and by now had recovered his senses and gotten to his feet, though his left arm was limp at his side. Nutella was nowhere to be seen. She had probably backflipped out a back door shortly after GAS arrived—she had a habit of skedaddling whenever they showed up and started stunning people. Protestors and party guests not yet stunned were being questioned and, in some cases, cuffed, except for the MIPs, whose attorneys had already filed preemptive lawsuits for the inconvenience. The wealthiest and most fortunate, like John Johnjohnson and Name, were free to go. The much wealthier and even more fortunate real Avocado Queen, had she deigned to attend the party in the first place, would have been free to go as well.

Unfortunately, the much poorer Frank Harken was less fortunate and had to deal with GAS and an agitated Officer Gunner Claymore.[99]

---

[99] You would be correct to point out that *agitated* is redundant here. Claymore only ever had one mood.

Frank Harken and I had both been temporarily incapacitated. He was now recovering and partially capacitated, with a hurt shoulder but otherwise upright and seemingly okay. I was once again fully operational and still invulnerable, like a battle station without any pesky exhaust ports wide open to a lucky shot by a whiny farm boy. It wasn't clear what had gone wrong with me, or why, but my systems were back running normally. I lifted the remnant of the giganticest perfume bottle off of my not-head and let it fall to the floor next to me. I didn't have a scratch. But my hat! My fedora, the wonderful eight-day-iversary present I'd received from myself that morning, was ruined! It was on top of my not-head when 800 pounds fell on me, and unlike me, it was not made of an indestructible alloy. The hat was crushed beyond all recognition. It wasn't a hat any longer. It might have been a good place mat. Or a bad frisbee. I started a background diagnostic to be sure whatever caused my malfunction would not do so again and went to assist my partner. "How are you? Does your arm hurt?"

He shrugged, which made him wince. "I think I'm still alive, though my shoulder's seen better days."

"This will help." I handed him a special[100] brew.

"What the hell happened?"

"Nutella was disguised as Avocado Queen. When the bottle fell, she blasted me into you and knocked you clear."

"I know. I was there, managed to see that much. I haven't lost my memory—you didn't hit me in the head. But how did the bottle fall? And why? And how come you didn't stop it?"

I told Harken I had temporarily malfunctioned, which elicited a pensive, "Hmm." As he contemplated the how and why and how come and sipped his coffee, Officer Claymore came over to us with a full head of steam. Almost literally—if you looked hard enough and had a little imagination, you could see it coming out of his ears despite the absence of vapebots. "Damn it, Harken, I told you no shenanigans!"

"Shenanigans? What're you talking about, Claymore? I didn't cause any shenanigans."

"You and this appliance are always up to something! How'd the coffeemaker end up under that giant bottle?"

"It was mostly because of physics," I said.

Claymore put his hand up to silence me. "I don't talk to appliances. Well, Harken, what do you have to say for yourself?"

Two could play that game. "I don't have anything to say for myself. What do you have to say for yourself?"

"I'm the one asking the questions here."

"Have you considered asking better ones? Like, why did that giant bottle fall over in the first place?"

"I don't need detective lessons from you," Claymore said.

---

[100] You could say all my brews are special, but then *special* would mean *regular*, which isn't especially special. It would be better to say all my brews are superb, which they are, and some of them are special, like this one was.

"I'm not teaching beginner classes, anyway. How about you let me take a look at that bottle so we can figure out what happened?"

"This is official GAS business. We don't let just anyone mess with the forensic evidence."

I tried to be helpful. "Excuse me, Mr. Officer, Sir, but Frank Harken isn't just anyone. He's a famous detective."

This pushed Claymore over the edge. He was dangling from a precipice, clinging to the cliffside with one sweaty, slippery hand. "I said I don't talk to appliances!"

Harken was pretty close to the edge himself, though his hiking boots had excellent traction and he didn't lose his balance or fall next to Claymore. (I hope I haven't confused you with my extending of the metaphor. Harken wasn't wearing hiking boots. Neither Harken nor Claymore were on a cliff. We were all still at OceanLand.) "Look, Claymore, it was my head that bottle almost fell on, not yours. I'm not gonna just stand around while you glorified security guards twiddle your thumbs."

"Security guards? You'd better watch your mouth. I don't know what strings you pulled last time to keep me from hauling you to the food court. I spent three hours in that elevator.[101] Three hours! I don't care who you know, keep pushing and I'm gonna push back."

"Strings? I didn't pull any strings. I don't know what you're talking about."

"Sure, Harken, sure. It must have been a coincidence that I was ordered to leave you alone."

Harken probably would have retorted something witty if the GAS forensics team hadn't called over to Claymore, "Chief! Come see this!"

I didn't know if *Chief* was an official title or a term of endearment. Either way, Claymore responded to it immediately

---

[101] Spoiler alert! (Don't be mad at me. After all my reminders, it's your own fault if you haven't already read *The Great American Deception*.)

and left us to see whatever *this* was. Harken and I followed. We were also interested in learning more about *this*.

This was inside the base of the giganticest perfume bottle, which was cracked all the way across. There was a mechanism implanted within, equipped with a saw, a chisel, a rubber mallet, right along the horizontal crack. It was mounted to the inside floor of the bottle and sat on a mobile pedestal. Someone could have been controlling it remotely to cut any side of the bottle at any height and angle. Someone must have been—without a doubt, the cut was deliberate. The falling bottle was not a materials failure, not an accident. Also, someone either had very bad aim, and missed Sannien by thirty-eight feet, or had very good aim, and didn't miss Frank Harken at all. Was he the intended target? Harken was alive only because of Nutella's astounding reflexes and perfect aim (and my hard not-head). All I could conclude for sure was there was definitely[102] a someone involved.

Harken might have been thinking these same thoughts while he silently leaned from behind Claymore to get a better look inside the bottle. I couldn't read his mind due to my lack of telepathic powers. It seems likely he was, though, since it's what I was thinking, and he was even a better detective than I was. On one of the other hands, he was focusing intently on the forensic evidence at that moment and, despite being a great detective, had a human brain that would be challenged to do two things at once. Though in that case it should be noted that the one thing his brain was doing, it was doing quite well: Harken got my attention and pointed at the bottom of the cutting mechanism's pedestal. It was hard to see it if you didn't have the eyes, focus, and brain of a great detective. (Fortunately, Harken had all of those, and not in jars on a high shelf where they wouldn't do him any good.) Snagged on the mechanism's multidirectional swivel, tucked underneath and almost out of

---

[102] *Sure* and *definitely* mean the same thing in this sentence and I could remove one of them, but if I did, would you know just how certain I was?

view, was a torn piece of fabric, a familiar shimmering dark blue.

We got out of there fast. Claymore was still consulting with forensics about the mechanism inside the perfume bottle when Harken and I hurried out of OceanLand. My partner finished his coffee as we caught the tram. He rotated his left shoulder without wincing and thanked me. "That was some cup of coffee." It's true. It was.

I didn't ask him where we were going because I had deduced that already. Harken didn't tell me where we were going because he had deduced that I had deduced that already. We were both detectives, you know. The shimmering dark blue fabric caught in the mechanism at the scene of the attempted crime wasn't the kind you see every day. Unless you happened to be a certain ventriloquist, in which case you would see it whenever you looked in the mirror or at your dummy, Annie. When we arrived, the front door of Dummy Academy was not only unlocked but also ajar.[103] We went in.

The room was a mess. When we'd visited earlier in the day, everything had been neatly put away in its appropriate container or bin. Now, all the ventriloquism props and outfits were scattered about the floor across the back of the room, like someone had gone through the bins in a frenzy and thrown everything blindly over their shoulder. Comically large eating utensils. Wilting flower. Swords. Guitar. Yo-yo. Magic wand. Chainsaw. Saxophone. Boxing gloves. Cowboy hat. Bathrobe. Tutu. Tuxedo. Anything a dummy or ventriloquist might wear or hold in a performance. There were also stage backdrops strewn across tables and on the floor. The large sheets with painted scenes that could hang from hooks behind the performer included a city skyline, snowcapped mountain range,

---

[103] This word means *open*, in case you didn't know. Also, I don't have to make every pun that pops into your head. I am capable of self-restraint.

GAS station holding cell, outer space with planets and stars, mini-golf course, and desert with very large cactuses.

The backdrop and props on the small black stage, however, were not a mess. Hanging neatly was a forest scene, thick with trees. On the folding chair in the center of the stage were three props side by side: an oversized magnifying glass, a coffee mug, and a fedora. There was nothing else on the stage. Harken and I just stared for a moment. I spoke first. "That's a funny coincidence. Until a little while ago I was wearing a fedora. And I'm a coffeemaker. And we're detectives."

He looked at me in that way he had of looking at me. "You know how I feel about coincidences. This isn't one. It's a clue, a message for us. A pretty blatant one."

I had been a detective for eight days, but I wasn't sure what the message was. Luckily, Harken had been a detective forever and knew what it meant. Even luckier for you and me both, he wasn't opposed to a little spoken exposition if it would help make sense of the plot.

"Margoria Magnificent was here in her teaching studio. Or maybe she was in her housing unit. Either way, she was feeling down, probably—tonight being Sannien's big party. She must've heard about it, might've been dwelling on how he was doing so well without her. Maybe some people she knows from their time together were going to be attending. So, she's alone, feeling left out. It's possible she connects with them to find out how it's going. Or possibly she doesn't—instead she keeps her mind off the party by preparing lessons for her next day of classes. At the party, the giant bottle of perfume falls, I'm almost killed, and Sannien loses a tail. Then we spot a shimmering piece of dark blue fabric, the exact fabric both Margoria and her dummy wear whenever they're performing, which is pretty much all the time. We put it together faster than anyone else, rush out of there to find her. Even though they're slower, GAS figures it out soon after—they're probably on their way here now. It isn't a very subtle clue, any idiot could figure it out, even Claymore. Some party guests see it too—they might even be the ones who point out to GAS that it's the exact material she always wears.

130

Someone there is friends with Margoria, or at least knows her, so they connect to her to warn her that we're coming. That GAS is coming. Whatever it is, she knows that they're coming for her, and that we're coming, too. She can't stay in her housing unit, if that's where she is—GAS would arrest her immediately. So, in a panic she rushes here, if she wasn't here already—knowing it's one of the first places we'll look—digs through ventriloquism props to send us a message, then hides somewhere. The coffee mug, magnifying glass, hat, that's us. The forest backdrop, that's where she wants us to go."

"You got all that from props on a chair and a backdrop?"

"None of this is subtle, Arjay. I wouldn't be much of a detective if I didn't get all that."

I ignored this insult, which strongly implied that I wasn't much of a detective. "That bottle of Sannien's Smell almost killed you. If a piece of her dress snagged on it when she was setting it up, then she had something to do with trying to kill you, right? Why would she tell us where to go? Why would we go? Could it be a trap?"

"Could be, but I don't think so. I think she wants our help."

"Why would we help her?"

"Maybe we know she had nothing to do with that bottle falling over."

"Do we know that?"

"A clue as blatant as a recognizable piece of fabric that clearly ties a suspect to the bottle, it's too easy. If Margoria is savvy enough to program, install, and control the mechanism that made the bottle fall, surely she's savvy enough not to wear her trademark blue dress while doing so or leave behind such an obvious clue. I doubt she had anything to do with the mechanism in the first place—it's a very sophisticated piece of equipment, not something most ventriloquists would know how to set up. But someone wants everyone to think she did it. She's being framed."

"Why? Who's framing her?"

Harken took down the forest backdrop and tossed it along with the magnifying glass, coffee mug, and fedora into the mess of other props. "That's what I don't know. Whoever it is, they're the one I want to talk to about that bottle that almost crushed me. Maybe Margoria can shed some light on it. That's why we're going to the Treeseeum like she instructed."

When we exited Dummy Academy, Gunner Claymore and his GAS officers were approaching. They might not have been the sharpest tools in the shed—besides that, the tools might have had flaking bits of rust and handles about to fall off, and the shed probably had a leaky roof—but even Claymore would have spotted the blue fabric caught in the mechanism, eventually. In this case, *eventually* had apparently been just minutes after we'd left. Someone at the party—maybe Sannien himself—must have recognized the fabric and made the connection to Margoria. It was easy. After all, Harken had said, that's why the fabric was there in the first place—to be seen, to be recognized, to establish her involvement in making the bottle fall, to send authorities after her. Harken was sure of it. He had learned over the years to trust his detective instincts, and they were telling him Margoria was innocent. We ducked behind a fountain and watched GAS enter Dummy Academy. They wouldn't learn anything looking at props all scattered on the floor. We were the only ones who had seen the clues pointing us to the Treeseeum.

We felt pretty clever as we walked away, having avoided being spotted by GAS and leaving them no clue to Margoria's whereabouts. We felt less clever, however, when we noticed two sport-coat guys trailing us as we headed to the shuttle. That's when we remembered that Tommy Ten-Toes had a personal interest in keeping Sannien safe, that he wanted the name of the person behind the threats to the influenceleb. By now he probably knew that Sannien had one tail less than he'd had earlier. And he also probably knew that Margoria Magnificent was the prime suspect. Lots of people knew by now—the blue fabric had given her away. What Ten-Toes didn't have was a location. Hence the sport-coats following us. They weren't exactly ninjas blending into the shadows. Harken and I cut through a crowded food court and lost them.

When we exited the shuttle, two new sport-coat guys were waiting for us. Ten-Toes didn't literally have eyes everywhere, but he did have eyes in lots of places. We were discovering that his network of gluten dealers was much larger than we would have guessed. When we gave the first sport-coats the slip, a dealer must have spotted us on the shuttle and relayed our location to other sport-coats. The sport-coats made no attempt to hide. Why would they? They didn't rely on stealth. They relied on superior numbers and surveillance. If we gave them the slip, another pair would find us.

Harken said that minutes counted and glanced at his watch. "Damn it!" He shook his wrist. It was broken! (The watch, not his wrist.) When I'd slammed into him at OceanLand and nearly broken his arm and shoulder, I'd more than nearly broken his watch. He shook his head, sighed, and then got back to business. Even without a working watch, Harken knew that minutes counted. We had to find Margoria before GAS did if we wanted to know what she knew. And we had to find her before Ten-Toes did if we wanted to know what she knew and to keep her safe— he blamed her for damaging his two-tailed marketing plan and might not be gentle about expressing his disapproval. Harken wasn't buying the whole I'm-just-a-legitimate-entertainment- business-mogul-and-not-a-feared-crime-boss rebrand Ten- Toes was selling. He was still very dangerous. Whoever was responsible for slicing Sannien's tail would learn that the hard way. We had good reason to avoid leading sport-coat goons right to Margoria, but couldn't waste time evading sport-coats just to have more sport-coats follow us just to evade them again in an endless cycle of sport-coat tag. So, we didn't try to give them the slip. They wanted to follow us, we'd let them follow us.

The Treeseeum was a living museum of trees. You wanted to see some trees, you paid the entry fee[104] and you could see 'em. You also could see real trees in other parts of the Great American, of course. Common areas and thoroughfares got plenty of sunlight and small trees in planters were standard décor in many neighborhoods. Individual attractions also used real trees when it fit the theme or provided appropriate ambience. But more often than not, simulated trees served the purpose just fine and required less upkeep. When you saw a tree, it wasn't always a tree. In any case, there were few places to experience being in a forest. Gravel paths from multiple entrances led to sections of trees, acres of maples, oaks, cedars, pines, poplars, birches. I could keep going and list every kind of

---

[104] Not a dollar and a half because dollars had no value in the Great American, or anywhere else, really.

tree to see in the Treeseeum, but is that how you want to spend the rest of your day? Just know that there were lots of kinds of trees, and lots of trees of each kind.

Each section of kinds of trees was a mini forest, with no gravel path within. A sign in the ground told you what kind of trees the section had. For example, one sign we passed said *Maple*. This made me think of the helpful syrupbots we'd seen back at Al the griddle pan's pancake-making demonstration. Did the syrup they dispensed come from similar trees? I suppose that had nothing to do with the current stage of our adventure, but it might help you appreciate the interconnectedness of all life. Or it might not.

The Treeseeum occupied all four levels of what would normally be the shopping district common area and stores, stretched far further than any ordinary neighborhood. It could take an hour to walk the length, much longer if you stopped to climb a tree or hug it or count all the leaves on a towering maple (which I definitely did not do, I promise. Do you know how long it takes to count 203,614 leaves?). Most people shuttled past the Treeseeum, because they thought looking up at trees was boring. Above the top of the trees, the ceiling was also the roof, linked atriums 200 feet high, providing full sun during the day and, without artificial lighting of any kind, at night providing only darkness.

Darkness was no problem for me. I didn't need light to see. Harken had human eyes, however, so I shone a light ahead to help him avoid walking into a tree. How embarrassing it would be for him to walk into a tree branch in the middle of working on a case! If it happened—and I'm not saying it did—it's definitely the sort of detail I'd have to include in my true account of our adventure. There's no way I'd leave that out. The Treeseeum was mostly empty as we continued walking and Harken rubbed the bruise on his forehead. If only he'd been wearing a hat, he might have had some head protection for any collision[105] that did or did not occur. Maybe I should've gotten him the deerstalker after all. How was I to know we'd end up in the woods?

We passed two tents and a group of people toasting s'mores around a firepit at a campsite. Camping was permitted in approved locations of the Treeseeum if you paid the fee and had a permit. For an upcharge, the Treeseeum would supply mosquitos and annoying tiny gnats.[106] The campers had ordered the premium package that included these insect pests as well as ticks. I didn't know if they'd paid the super-premium for a chance of getting Lyme disease. Sadly, the bear-mauling simulation was down for maintenance, so campers couldn't experience the full pleasures of the great outdoors. Still, all connections were blocked in the forest, and people couldn't play lens games or message friends or rate pics of what strangers were having for dinner. To entertain themselves, they had to resort to singing songs around a campfire and possibly talking to each other, proving it was still possible to rough it in the Great American.

When we left the path, the forest floor was too thick with branches and leaves and pinecones (where applicable) for my wheels. However, my tank treads trod over them easily, much like you'd expect tank treads to trod. This was the first time in my account of our true adventures that I'd had the opportunity to use my tank treads, for those keeping track of such things. Two parallel, wide, oblong sets of treads on a quick swivel let me traverse uneven terrain and make sharp turns even when off the

---

[105] There used to be a different word, *allision*, for when a moving object like a person's head smashed into a stationary object like a tree, as opposed to two moving objects colliding with each other (it was usually applied to ships on the seas rather than heads into trees). However, for a long time most people didn't note the distinction and whenever anything hit anything, it was a *collision*.

[106] On a previous case, Tommy Ten-Toes had threatened to squash Harken like a "tiny gnat." No relation to the ones in the Treeseeum, probably.

beaten path. We were deeper in the woods now, far from the campsite and the singing campers, and the path was undefeated. Harken saw a sign indicating tropical trees were coming up, and knew we were approaching Margoria.

Two sport-coats were still behind us, forty-three yards. Harken had had about enough of them following us. "I've had about enough of them following us," he said, which is how I knew. "Can you immobilize them?" He knew I could, of course. There was no need for me to reply. He followed his rhetorical-question-that-was-really-a-request with a bit of direction. "Don't cause permanent damage. In case you were thinking of using your vibrational saw on their legs."

"Got it," I said, and immediately canceled my plan to use my vibrational saw and formulated a new plan that entailed less horrified screaming. I'd say I turned on a dime, but the only dimes in the Great American were in monetary museums. There were certainly none to be found on a forest floor in the Treeseeum. Coins and paper money were as obsolete as whatever other items you can think of that are no longer used. In the old days outside, people would say they turned on a dime. They would also say they stopped on a dime. Dimes were small. You were considered quite maneuverable and agile if you could do things like turn or stop in the tiny space they occupied. If you could do both at the same time, that might be even more impressive. I could do both at the same time and did, veering around an elm tree and heading straight for the men wearing sport coats.

I suppose one reason for always wearing a sport coat is to hide your shoulder-holstered handgun. They drew their weapons when they saw me coming. Don't worry! Bullets couldn't scratch my impenetrable shell. Couldn't penetrate it either. Bullets, however, could ricochet and damage a person or, worse, a tree. I communicated with the guns' protective biometric sensing feature, the one that only lets the weapon shoot if the trigger is being pressed by the authorized user. When informed that an unauthorized person was holding the gun, the trigger locked and the gun refused to fire. Both men looked down at their weapons. As authorized persons holding their own guns, they were not expecting this. By the time they looked back up, I was upon them. Not literally. I didn't run over the sport-coat guys. I did snatch and disassemble their weapons before they knew what was happening. That wasn't difficult. Most henchpersons rarely knew what was happening. It was part of the job description.

While they stood dumbfounded,[107] I brewed a couple of coffees and handed them over. The sport-coat guys held the coffees they hadn't asked for. "Drink up!" I said. They hesitated, understandable considering how dumbfounded they were. In the Great American, bots didn't tell humans what to do. Bots followed orders, completed tasks that didn't require actual thought, and spoke, if they spoke at all, following preprogrammed speech coding. Mostly, in the shopping and residential districts, bots helped people vape or bet or pick up dog poop or consume cocktail weenies or other things. They weren't permitted in roles like bartending or waiting tables or dentistry—people generally didn't like too much direct bot interaction, possibly because of some violent high-profile malfunctions and hacking incidents many years earlier, possibly because many people feared losing customer-service jobs to superior bot efficiency, possibly because some people still told stories of being beaten by copbots on the outside. Most Great American bots stayed on the garden level basement and manufactured and assembled, their intelligence and autonomy strictly limited. Most Great American bots certainly didn't charge at people and demand they drink coffee.

I wasn't most Great American bots. "Drink up!"

"But I'm not thirsty," one sport-coat said. His tone wasn't tough-henchperson. It was non-tough pleading. I recognized both of the men. They were at GASP[108] during our first case eight days earlier, had experienced firsthand what I was capable

---

[107] Not that different from slack-jawed and dumbstruck.
[108] The Great American Stargazer Panorama.

of. One still had a bandage on his wrist, the other a slightly bruised cheekbone that hadn't fully healed.

"Drink up!" I said. When they hesitated again, I told them we could do this the easy way or the hard way, a helpful persuasion tactic I'd learned from friendly bowling alley bouncers. Unlike the bouncers, I was specific. The hard way, I informed my sport-coated friends, entailed a vibrational saw and terrible pain and suffering. The easy way entailed very tasty coffee and a painless, short nap. They had three seconds to choose. By the time I'd counted aloud to two, they were drinking with an enthusiasm that bordered on eagerness. Seven seconds later they were asleep on the forest floor, drooling a little but still in possession of all their limbs and major internal organs. Minor ones as well, in case any of those mattered.

I caught up to Harken, who was now on the gravel path heading to tropical hardwoods. Just before the beginning of the section of teak trees, we came to a fork in the path. The fork was three feet long and plastic, with four tines, a ventriloquist's prop that was sure to cause uproarious laughter and shocked gasps when a dummy said, "That's forking huge!" and used "fork" in other clever sentences that invited profane interpretation. It's what made a giant fork one of the funniest props. According to 91% of ventriloquists, it was even funnier than a big cork. There wasn't one of those on the gravel path, but there were large plastic flowers, a set of bright, multicolored dahlias. To be sure we wouldn't misunderstand the meaning and purpose of the props, there was also a garden spade and, leaning against a tree at the edge of the path, a small flashing sign that said *These Are Clues*. Even before he saw the helpful sign, Harken knew the props were clues. He deserved his fame as a great detective. He turned off the flashing sign, folded it, and put it in his pocket, trashed the fork, flowers, and gardening spade so no one else would discover where we were heading next, and off we headed.

The Garden of Forking Paths was a garden. That's part of how it got its name. It was also a labyrinth, which is part of why its paths were described as forking. The other part of why the paths were described as forking and also how the garden got its name was that it contained thirty-two tapas[109] shacks along the maze, all offering delectable a la carte selections. Hungry maze walkers traditionally brought their own forks to taste delicious morsels while trying to navigate the labyrinth, which could take up to seven hours if they wanted to find and sample from every eatery before exiting. It's true that some of the tapas could be eaten without a fork, but no one thought to call the place the Garden of Forking and Sometimes Using Your Hands Paths. That name was accurate enough, but didn't roll off the tongue.

Authentic-seeming, synthetic, opaque hedges on both sides created paths that made up the maze. The hedges were in six-foot-long sections on hidden tracks and hinges and rotated and shifted unpredictably at irregular intervals. You could be on the right path, about to reach the tapas shack you were trying to find, and suddenly find yourself in a dead end. You might wait for the hedges to switch back again, but given that there were 24,955 hedges and if not an actual infinite variety of possible labyrinthian combinations, nonetheless a number higher than humans could count without computational assistance, it was wiser to accept the new maze and keep moving. The Garden of Forking Paths, like life, was all about finding a different way to reach the tapas shack with tasty morsels rather than holding out hope for the old path to return.[110]

---

[109] *Tapas* might have originally referred to appetizer-like, shareable Spanish food, from Spain. In the Great American, it eventually had its meaning expanded to refer to similarly served food from other Spanish-speaking countries, including Argentina, which was the variety of food served in the Garden of Forking Paths, for reasons that might or might not be obvious.

[110] In case you were looking for some profound meaning hidden in the true account of our adventures.

Unlike the Treeseeum, the Garden of Forking Paths didn't prevent people from connecting. Lots of people used nav to make their way through the maze, though maze-walking purists looked down on that. Purists also judged people harshly for rushing through without finding and eating at all thirty-two shacks. Harken said we didn't have time for that, which was fine with me because I don't eat, something I might have mentioned before. He said we were on a case and minutes counted, though sadly he couldn't glance at a working wristwatch while saying it, like he usually did. It was unlikely a sports-coat lackey or gluten dealer working for Ten-Toes would just happen to be in the labyrinth and just happen upon Margoria. Still, the longer it took us to find her, the greater the chances they or GAS would get a ping and snag her first. If that happened to happen, how would we ask her important questions like *Did you try to kill Frank Harken?* and *If not, do you know who did?* and *Why would someone want to frame you?* and *This might be a little off topic, but where can we get one of those giant forks?*

It was no help that my spatial sensors made navigating the labyrinth easy—hedges could shift position all they wanted, and I could access overhead security cams and instantly determine the new quickest way to the exit or to any of the thirty-two tapas shacks all I wanted, and that wouldn't get us any closer to finding Margoria Magnificent. We had no idea where she was. How lucky for us that she knew exactly where we were. Eight hedges shifted to surround us in a twelve-by-twelve square with no exit. Then the floor beneath us descended. It was a circular lift that had blended into the rest of the floor seamlessly. There weren't any seams—even I hadn't detected it. We were lowered into a narrow tunnel, with white cinderblock walls, soft lights, and a ceiling high enough for Harken to stand up straight. After we stepped off the lift, it lifted itself back into position. The hedges were probably already shifting in the Garden of Forking Paths above, eliminating the square that had surrounded us and becoming just another path in the ever-changing maze.

We almost didn't recognize Margoria standing in the tunnel ahead. She wore a Groucho fake nose-mustache-glasses and so did Annie the dummy. That might explain why the peacegrid and gluten dealers hadn't spotted her when she'd traveled from Dummy Academy to the Treeseeum, and from there to the Garden of Forking Paths. Ventriloquism props were more versatile than most people would have guessed, if it were something they ever thought about at all. Margoria and Annie weren't wearing their signature blue shimmering dresses, either. They were in matching lavender jumpsuits.

"Thank goodness you're here," Margoria said.

"Goodness had nothing to do with it," Harken said. "Someone almost killed me today."

"It wasn't me! You must believe that." She backed away from him.

He didn't pursue her, put his hands up as reassurance that he wasn't angry. "I know it wasn't you."

"Thank goodness," she said again, and started to quietly cry. "When I heard that Saney lost his tail, that they thought I did it, I panicked."

"For a panicked person, you did a hell of a job leaving us clues about where to go."

"Tonya connected from the party, told me about Saney's tail, about the bottle almost hitting you, about the fabric from my dress they found. She said right after you left, GAS officers said my name and left too. I knew they were coming to arrest me. I figured you'd go to Dummy Academy to find me, wanted to wait for you there so I could ask for your help. No one's going to believe I had nothing to do with it. I needed a detective who could uncover what had really happened. I don't know any detectives besides you. But I decided it was too risky to stay— what if GAS got there before you did? You couldn't help me if I was taken to a jail cell and we never talked. I had to hide. Where could I go? How could I get you to find me?"

Harken wasn't going to be out-expositioned by a ventriloquist. "And then you remembered that you'd told me about the time you took Sannien to the Treeseeum to see the teak trees. So you put up a forest backdrop and props so we'd know it was a message for us about where to find you. Why didn't you wait at the teak trees?"

"Just as I'd finished setting up the props to send you to the Treeseeum, another friend at the party connected to tell me a bunch of men in sport coats had gone running out of OceanLand. She overheard one of them say my name. I didn't know who they were, but I realized it wasn't just GAS after me for what had happened to Saney, and then I realized the Tree-seeum was too dangerous. It has no connections or cameras. What if the sport-coated men found me there before you did? They could kill me and no one would know. I decided the Garden of Forking Paths was a safer meeting spot. There wasn't time to set the stage up to send you there—I imagined GAS or sport-coated men would show up at Dummy Academy any second and catch me, so I grabbed other props as fast as I could and headed to the Treeseeum to leave clues there for you. Stayed in the teak forest just long enough for that and then came here. I guess I was hoping that making it complicated would give you an edge, that since you're a detective, you'd find me before they would."

"And why here?"

"The Garden of Forking Paths? That's easy. I recently started working here part time, cooking tapas, and have access to the employee tunnels beneath the maze. Workers can't spend hours trying to find tapas shacks through the maze every time they come to work, so we use the tunnels that lead to each shack. I have a friend working the maze tonight, asked for his help. It seemed like the safest place to go."

"Dummy Academy not doing enough business?"

"Barely hanging on. I don't know how long I'll be able to keep it going. A VentriloQuest franchise just moved into the next neighborhood."

Just then two cooks walked past us in the tunnel. Margoria nodded hello to them. She was still wearing her Groucho glasses-nose-mustache and holding Annie, similarly disguised.

Harken thought the whole thing was overly complicated and maybe not the most brilliant plan. "We can't stay here long.

Isn't there some record of you working here? Won't GAS figure that out?"

Annie responded, "She told you already, she panicked. It was all she could think to do. Where else can we go?"

Harken put a finger up to the dummy's lips, silencing it. "First, I need information. If you didn't try to kill me, who did?"

"I don't know," Margoria said.

"Why would someone want to frame you?"

"I don't know."

"What's the deal with you and Sannien?"

"I already told you about that. We dated for a few months and then he decided he liked someone else."

"What are you leaving out?"

Annie encouraged her. "Go ahead, tell him."

That gave Margoria strength. "For a while, I've been sending Saney... pics."

"Pics?"

"Pics. To remind him of what he's missing."

"And?"

"And what?"

"What did he say?"

"Nothing. He hasn't responded. Which surprised me, because, well, these are not the kind of pics Saney would ignore, if you know what I mean."

"Okay," Harken said.

"I mean, they're not the kind of pics you'd send your parents." She didn't wink at him, but she might as well have.

"I think I get the idea."

"They were very dirty."

"Yes, yes. I understand."

"Like, in one pic—"

"—Ms. Magnificent, please, I don't want any details about the pics you sent. Just tell me what happened when Sannien didn't respond."

"I kept sending them."

"And?"

"And then I got a threatening message. An anonymous one. If I didn't stop sending pics to Saney, I'd regret it."

"Who sent the message?"

"I don't know," she said.

To be helpful, I added, "That's what *anonymous* means."

"Not now, Arjay. Could it be The Juggler? Maybe he caught wind[111] of the pics and got jealous, worried you'd steal Sannien back? Threatened you to get you to back off?"

"I don't know."

"Did you stop sending pics?"

"No, I kept sending them. Saney hasn't responded, but I know he will. He just needs time. He'll come to his senses. I switched my inbox to private, blocked messages from anyone who wasn't a friend. I haven't been threatened since. That was a week ago."

"So someone could still be sending you threats. You're just not receiving them?"

Margoria and Annie both shrugged. "I guess."

"Hmm," Harken said, which is what he sometimes said when he was thinking. "We don't know if the threat's connected to you being framed. And we don't know how any of that connects to someone dropping a giant bottle on my head. What we do know is we aren't gonna get answers here in tunnels beneath the Garden of Forking Paths. What's the best way out of here? I'd like to talk to Sannien."

"I would, too, but what about GAS? What about the men in sport coats?"

Harken assured her that we could handle them. "We'll keep you safe and find out what's really going on."

His confidence made Margoria feel less afraid, a feeling that lasted a long time, all the way until we exited the Garden of Forking Paths and were met by Tommy Ten-Toes, Iceberg, and forty-one lackeys in sport coats.

---

[111] Pics could be scented and often were.

At the end of the winding employee tunnel beneath the Garden of Forking Paths, we stepped onto a lift and seconds later found ourselves back on the shopping level, in a dead-end alley next to the attraction's delivery entrance. There weren't any shops or kiosks in the alley, just some maintenance equipment and crates of restaurant supplies waiting to be unpacked. In addition, there were Tommy Ten-Toes, Iceberg, and forty-one lackeys in sport coats. It's possible you know this last part already, since I told you in the cliffhanger ending to the previous chapter. Even the unreliable memory of a human should be sufficient for you to still recall it now. I hope this sophisticated narrative tactic of mine is helping you to experience an appropriate level of suspense. Not so little that you fall asleep, and not so much that you get anxious, especially if you have high blood pressure or a weak heart.

It was late, approaching one in the morning, but non-technically it was still the same day as it was when the case began. Ten-Toes was handsome as ever, still wore his lightning bolt pinstriped suit, still had a pink stargazer pinned to his lapel, still had his arm in a sling. Iceberg still wore the world's largest [112] white tuxedo and bow tie, still had shoulder hair fighting its way out the top of his collar, still had pure arctic eyes that you could get lost in if you liked that sort of thing and had a bad sense of direction. Sport-coat lackeys still wore sport coats and generic faces not worth describing. They stood in a semicircle facing us. Iceberg and Ten-Toes stepped forward.

Margoria shrank back. It was her first encounter with a feared-crime-boss-turned-wildly-successful-entrepreneur.

Ten-Toes took another step toward us. "Surprised to see me, detective?"

Harken didn't shrink back. Or anywhere else. "Actually, yes, I am. How'd you find us?"

"It wasn't hard, really. The young man operating the maze tonight happens to be one of my gluten dealers. He spotted you when you showed up."

Margoria let out an anguished shriek. She'd been betrayed by a friend, a coworker, a person of low character who apparently had no sense of labyrinthian comradery. Annie shrieked as well.

Harken took a diagonal step toward Ten-Toes, blocking Margoria from his view. "Is there anyone who doesn't deal gluten for you?"

"What can I say? I employ a lot of people."

"I guess we should thank you for doing your part for the economy."

"You're welcome."

Harken didn't like so much small talk. "What do you want?"

Instead of answering, Ten-Toes expressed his disappointment. "Detective, you were supposed to keep Sannien safe. You failed miserably. He had two tails earlier today and now he has one. That's half as many tails. [113] How is he supposed to promote

---

[112] Unofficial. Global data was not available.
[113] You don't become a wildly successful entrepreneur without knowing how to do math.

my new business venture with only one tail? Are teens even going to listen to him now? You don't have a smart answer for that, do you? Well, at least you caught the perpetrator in record time. You can hand her over to me."

Margoria shrank back even further.

"Ten-Toes, she had nothing to do with Sannien losing a tail."

"I might not be a detective, but I know evidence when I see it. They found a piece of her dress in the bottle."

"I know. I was there. It was my head that bottle almost fell on. And I'm telling you she had nothing to do with it. It was a setup."

"And how do you know that?"

"Call it a hunch."

"A hunch?"

"His hunches are quite reliable," I said.

My entering the conversation made some of the sport-coats nervous. During our first case, a few of them had been on the receiving end of, well, me. Others had heard about it from injured coworkers. I was developing quite a rep.[114] Even Ten-Toes hesitated, if only for a moment. "We have overwhelming numbers. And we found our two missing men in the forest along with their disassembled weapons. Clever, messing with their guns' biometric identification feature so they wouldn't work. We've turned those off. Your coffeemaker isn't going to be able to stop us."

Harken shrugged, to convey that what I did was no concern of his and he just wanted everyone to know he couldn't be held responsible for any carnage that might result. "Are you sure about that?"

Clearly, Ten-Toes wasn't, but he wasn't the sort to back down. "Do you really want me as an enemy?"

---

[114] Which is short for *reputation*, though my explaining this has now made it long instead of short.

"I can't say that I do," Harken said. "Though I might ask you the same question. I don't know if Arjay can take out all of you. It might be fun to find out. What do you think, partner?"

"My calculations indicate possibly."

Ten-Toes laughed. "Detective, you're as stubborn as ever. Be reasonable. I'm sure we can work something out."

"I'm sure we can."

"I'll tell you what—you say she had nothing to do with the attack on Sannien; since you're such a great detective, that should be easy enough for you to prove. I'll hold onto her and she'll remain safe and secure. You go investigate and then give me the name of the person who's really to blame, and I let her go unharmed."

"Yeah, that's a hard pass. She stays with me."

Ten-Toes' eyes narrowed and his fists clenched. His voice stayed level, however. "All right, you win. She stays with you. My man Iceberg will stay with you as well, to make sure there's no funny business."[115]

"Absolutely not."

"I'm not asking. This is no longer a negotiation. Iceberg will accompany you. You get me the name of the real culprit and she'll have nothing to worry about."

I couldn't see wheels moving in Harken's head, because I don't have X-ray vision and also the human head does not contain wheels. I could tell that he was weighing his options, figuring the odds. Should he push back at Ten-Toes and risk the situation escalating to immediate violence? Forty-one was a lot of lackeys, and I hadn't exactly given a guarantee that I could defeat them all. If we did manage to get away, there would be gluten dealers to spot us, and more sport-coats to deal with, and how would we solve this case if all our energies were spent evading and fighting Ten-Toes? Harken calculated correctly when he determined that the best move was to give in and reluctantly let Iceberg come with us.

---

[115] A difficult task, since this was our main kind of business.

As we walked out of the alley, Ten-Toes upped the stakes. "And detective, my patience has limits. You'll provide the name of the culprit by tomorrow, early afternoon. I have evening dinner plans I don't want interrupted."

Iceberg didn't say anything as we walked through Burnt Sienna Neighborhood 253. He hadn't argued with Tommy Ten-Toes when told to come with us, because, my impudent partner notwithstanding, people didn't argue with Tommy Ten-Toes. However, silent though he was, it was still clear Iceberg was less than pleased. I wasn't one to pry, but I was one to ask someone about whatever it was they didn't want to talk about.

"Iceberg, what are you upset about?"

"I'm not upset."

"Is it because coming with us means you'll have to do a lot of walking?" Iceberg was carrying around substantially more mass than most humans. It couldn't be easy on the knees.

"I don't mind walking," he said.

Harken said, "Someone should ask the floor how it feels about it."

"You are just hilarious," Iceberg said to my partner. "If you must know, it's your insensitive, sizephobic bullying I was not looking forward to."

"I don't must know. I didn't ask and I don't care."

"I asked," I said. It's true. I had.

"Thank you, Arjay. At least someone here is a decent person."

"I'm not a person, but you're welcome. I'm just happy the team is back together."

Harken didn't like that. "We're not a team. I mean, you and I are, of course, but not Iceberg. He works for Tommy Ten-Toes. Don't forget that."

"I know," I said, because I did. "But we had such fun together on our first case. Remember that time we got a ketchup pizza?"[116]

"We're on a case and minutes count. We don't have time for *This Is Your Life*."

When my partner started referring to television shows from the twentieth century, it was a sure sign he needed a coffee. I handed him one.

As we walked, Margoria Magnificent eyed Iceberg nervously. This was understandable since she was new to the whole walking-through-the-Great-American-with-a-humongous-enforcer sort of thing. Annie eyed him as well. It's true Annie didn't have working eyes, since she was a dummy made of wood, but it might be rude to keep bringing up her lack of being alive. She was doing her best with what she had. Besides, we all have our short-comings, humans most of all. (Nothing personal.)

We approached 347 people watching a qualifying round of championship mini-golf. The crowd favorite was Victory Winner, the twelve-year-old phenom who had taken the mini-golf world by storm. If that sounds like a cliché, it could be because you don't follow professional mini-golf very closely and are unaware that Victory's first major victory was at the blizzard tournament a month earlier. She'd played through snow-covered greens, gale force winds, and blinding snow squalls to blow away the competition, recording the lowest snowstorm score since the tournament's inception.

Today's qualifying round was not at a weather course. It was at a pirate course that consisted of two full-size pirate ships right there in the main thoroughfare, rocking back and forth in a small artificial lake and blasting each other with glitter cannons while actors dressed as pirates swashbuckled and fought choreographed battles with cutlasses. The ships shook with each cannon blast, which could make golf balls roll away from the hole. It was a timed competition—players didn't have

---

[116] Don't worry! No one in our group ate the culinary atrocity. It was actually an important clue for our first case.

the luxury of waiting for the distracting sword fight to end, but had to play through even as pirates shouted, "Shiver me timbers!" and glitter rained down. There were nine holes on each ship and golfers had to successfully swing on a rope across the gap between ships to continue playing the back nine.[117] Winner, playing like the winner she was, made short work of the eleventh hole despite a pirate's parrotbot trying to break her concentration by squawking pirate insults. Sinking a fourteen-foot putt while the whole ship of a golf course is rocking in the water and shaking from cannon blasts and a fake parrot is calling you a "lily-livered, scabby sea bass" requires exceptional skill and focus, but they wouldn't call her Victory Winner if she couldn't do it. Also, if she had a different name.

As the spectating crowd cheered for another victory, we left the mini-golf pirate ships behind and entered Yellow Neighborhood 220. It was a calming shade of mellow yellow because the entire neighborhood was a Maybe-Don't-Be-So-Loud zone. The nonstop stimulation of the Great American could be exhausting, which you might be experiencing for yourself by now, and some people wanted the nonstopping to at least pause once in a while. If they did, they could come to neighborhoods like this one and sit silently in a chair and watch paint dry. A dozen Adirondack chairs faced a twenty-by-twenty freshly painted canvas. No cheering or betting on the outcome was permitted, assuring peace and tranquility for those gazing absently at the solid square of gentle lilac. In case that was not enough, softly fluttering ludebots,[118] resembling pez dispensers with wings, offered little pills to help people relax. If watching

---

[117] The water between the ships contained no crocodiles making tick-tock clock noises, so players who fell would get wet but not eaten. Despite this, it was a popular mini-golf course.

[118] Not to be confused with lewdbots, which were not permitted in Maybe-Don't-Be-So-Loud zones due to their propensity for repeatedly yelling the kinds of words a bot with my refined sophistication would never say. They were most often used for desensitizing employees who were training to work on the sales floor with retail customers.

paint dry was too much stimulation, there were plenty of isolation chambers available for rent in ten-minute intervals. If your budget was tight, you could chip in on a group isolation chamber. It's true they weren't as isolated as the solitary isolation chambers, but they were every bit as much chambers.

Margoria Magnificent asked Harken where we were going and was immediately shushed by five professional shushers. Those who might have been librarians in an earlier era were in high demand in Maybe-Don't-Be-So-Loud zones.

Harken spoke softly. "First, far away from Ten-Toes before he changes his mind."

"What about him?" she quietly asked, nodding at the largest man she had ever seen.

"Iceberg? Don't be afraid of this big lug. He's mostly harmless. Practically a pet. He might as well be some variety of doodlepoo."

Iceberg spoke softly, too, though in his case that was always true. "You know, I'm walking right next to you. I can hear what you're saying."

"I didn't realize my hushed sounds reached that altitude."

"Great. More size jokes. You are wonderful to be around."

"I know," Harken said.

A moment earlier, Harken had said "first" we were going away from Ten-Toes, which might imply that he was soon going to tell Margoria where we were going second. And maybe he would have. We didn't get a chance to find out because that's when the attack occurred.

There were seven of them, all wearing T-shirts embossed with the words *Avenge the Tail*. They weren't armed, but any group of people who could organize themselves with matching custom-embossed shirts in such a short time was obviously quite dangerous. They had somehow located Margoria despite her Groucho nose-mustache-glasses. Maybe it had something to do with the dummy she was carrying. Sannien fans had probably connected pics of the suspect ventriloquist to each other, and since Annie was a dummy, she was recognizable even while wearing nose-mustache-glasses of her own.

What followed was not the most evenly matched fight in the history of pugilism. The Sannien superfans tried to grab Margoria. It wasn't clear what they were planning to do with her to achieve their tail vengeance, and they weren't given the opportunity to clarify. Harken immediately punched one of them in the eye, resulting in screaming that sounded a lot like, "Ow! My eye! My eye! My eye!" Harken then threw a forearm into another's jaw, resulting in no screaming at all because screaming while unconscious is difficult. He turned to deal with the others and saw they were already laid out on the floor, in varying degrees of pain.

Iceberg was a gentle soul and usually avoided violence, but when the other five tail avengers attempted to grab and possibly abscond with the ventriloquist his boss had ordered him to keep an eye on, he didn't have much choice. If you've ever seen an elephant trample a group of people, you have some idea how Iceberg handled them. If you haven't, good for you—it's a violent scene you're better off not having in your head. The big man straightened his bow tie.

During the brief but violent commotion, professional shushers had shushed us to no avail.

Margoria was frightened but unharmed. Annie was okay as well, just a little stiff, because she was made of wood.

"You're still blocking the peacegrid?" my partner asked.

"I'm obscuring passive identification to keep GAS from spying on us.[119] I can't prevent direct reports from individuals. A lot of people saw this. GAS will be here soon."

"Good."

"Good?" Margoria asked. "You want GAS to get me?"

"Margoria, I want you to stay safe and alive while I figure out what the hell is going on. I can't investigate this case and

---

[119] Something I had been unable to do with the network of gluten dealers, whose tech was triple-encrypted on a closed channel.

protect you from random attacks at the same time. Besides, the next attempt by Sannien's fans could be more sophisticated, or be a larger group. We might not be able to stop them. And now GAS is on their way. If we have to evade them as well as crazy fans—I'm not sure we can, and even if we somehow managed to, when will we be proving your innocence by finding the real perpetrator? We can't do it if we're on the run."

"Detective, what are you saying?"

"You'll be safe with GAS. They'll take you to a holding cell. No Sannien fanatics can get you there. We'll find out who framed you and have you freed before you know it."

"I don't want to go to jail."

"It isn't jail. It's a holding cell. I've been in a few myself. They're just holding you there. It's temporary."

We could see GAS officers approaching.

"Don't let them take me."

"Margoria, this is the only way. We'll have you out of there soon."

"Don't worry," I told her. "Frank Harken is a great detective. We'll solve this case."

That didn't make her feel better. I could tell Annie was also upset.

The arriving GAS squad was led by Officer Gunner Claymore, because of course it was.

"Harken," he shouted in that way he had of always shouting.

His squad of five officers kept their distance and aimed stunners at us. Claymore might have instructed them about how we disarmed his GAS officers during our first case when they got too close.[120] Unfortunately, I couldn't manipulate settings on GAS stunners the way I had with sport-coat guys' guns at the Treeseeum. And if I tried anything, they might stun Harken, leaving us with a sleeping, drooling detective to lead the way. Even if I did manage to take out the five officers before they could fire their stunners, doing so in public, while dozens of onlookers looked on and professional shushers shushed, was

---

[120] You probably already know all about it.

sure to cause more problems than we already had. More GAS officers would arrive with more stunners. We couldn't solve this case and free Margoria if we were in a holding cell with her. I'd correctly intuited my partner's sentiments—Harken gave me a look that told me to take no action as Claymore stepped forward.

Claymore was delighted. "I've got you now, Harken. Aiding and abetting."

"Aiding and abetting? Are you kidding me?"

"Not kidding even a little. It's a serious charge."

"It's a nonsense charge. I might have aided someone, but I certainly haven't abetted."

"I know what I see. You're protecting this fugitive from justice and helping her evade capture."

Harken indicated the tail avengers sprawled on the floor. "It's true we protected her from these lawless vigilantes. And now we're handing her over to you. Which is what we were on our way to do when they attacked."

"You expect me to believe you were bringing her to GAS? What do I look like, some kind of person who believes blatant lies?"

"Claymore, who is my client? Who did I tell you I was working for at the party?"

"I'll ask the questions here."

"Don't change the subject. You know who I was working for. Go ahead, it won't hurt you to say it."

Claymore disliked not being the one asking the questions and disliked his answer more. "Sannien. You said you were working for Sannien."

"And the tail this ventriloquist is accused of slicing off, who did it belong to?"

Claymore looked defeated as he answered, "Sannien."

"Exactly, and now, having apprehended the suspect in the attack on my client, I am turning her over to you. How is that abetting?"

"It just is!"

"Come on, Claymore. Even you know you have nothing on us."

"But you're here with the enforcer of a suspected former crime boss."

"Excuse me," Iceberg said, "My boss is a totally legitimate entertainment entrepreneur mogul. And I'm not an enforcer. As of yesterday, my official title is executive assistant."

"How exciting," I said. "Congratulations!"

Claymore looked from Iceberg to Harken. "I should bust you all down to the station."

"For what?" I asked.

Claymore's frustration hit a peak[121] and he shouted, "I don't talk to appliances!" He searched and failed to find some pretext to arrest or stun us. Finally, he ordered his officers to take Margoria into custody.

Harken put his hand up, cautiously, to get them to pause for a second. "Claymore, she's not guilty. I know what the evidence shows, I know you have to take her, but can you give me a few hours? Maybe process the paperwork slowly? I just need a little time to get the evidence to exonerate her."

Claymore more snarled than laughed. You might say he snarlghed if you can figure out how to pronounce it. "You want me to help you?"

"I want you to give the truth a chance. I want the same thing you want, justice."

"You don't tell me how to do my job. Step aside or get stunned."

Harken stepped aside.

As they cuffed Margoria (and Annie), she said, "Detective Harken, please don't let them take me."

"It'll be okay," he said.

"Promise. Promise you'll get me out."

Harken knew better than to promise. Great American justice could be fickle. But she pleaded again, and he wanted to comfort her. "I'll find out who framed you and get you out."

"Promise me."

---

[121] No relation to the metaphorical cliffside precipice he almost fell off at the party.

He hesitated.

"Promise me!"

Harken gave in. "I promise."

As GAS took Margoria away, Annie called back to Harken. "Remember, you promised. You promised. You promised."

"**Y**ou know," Iceberg said, "my boss is not going to be happy you let GAS take Margoria. How am I supposed to keep an eye on her now?"

"You know," Harken said, "I don't care if your boss is happy. If it makes you feel better, you can keep an eye on me. That's what Ten-Toes wanted anyway. Besides, there's no need to keep an eye on Margoria. She's innocent."

"If she didn't slice Sannien's tail, who did?"

"I don't know yet. That's going to require some detective work."

They were talking at regular volume because we were no longer in a Maybe-Don't-Be-So-Loud zone, which still meant Iceberg's voice was gentle and quiet. The way he talked, you might forget that he'd recently trampled five people, as long as you weren't one of them. "Being a detective seems interesting. I learned a lot on our last case. If I ever stop working for Ten-Toes, it might be a good career to try."

159

"There wasn't any *our* last case. You tagged along with us because Ten-Toes insisted. Just like this time. You're no detective. Stick to being an enforcer."

I pointed out that Iceberg was now officially an executive assistant. Iceberg thanked me. Then I asked my partner, "Do we have any suspects? Could John Johnjohnson or Name be the blackmailer? Do you think The Juggler is behind this?"

Harken thought for a moment. "I'm not sure Johnjohnson or Name could figure out how to blackmail someone even if they wanted to. Anyway, I'm thinking Sane Mama had a point when she asked how you blackmail someone who has no shame. If Sannien had done something horrible and people found out, it would probably just make him more popular. Besides, we still haven't seen any evidence of blackmail. That's why we're heading to talk to the famous man himself. If he's done crying over his tail, maybe he can shed some light on all of this. As for The Juggler, it's hard to see what his motive would be. I guess he could've found out about the pics Margoria was sending to Sannien and gotten jealous. But even if that could lead him to frame her, why in the world would he want to drop a bottle on my head and disrupt Sannien's new scent party? How does killing me figure into any of that?"

Iceberg ventured a guess. "You can be very abrasive. There are probably a lot of people who would be happy to see you dead. Maybe killing you has nothing to do with Margoria."

"Thanks for the astute detective work. Come to think of it, you're probably one of those people who'd be happy to see me dead. How do I know you didn't program the bottle to fall on me?"

"If I wanted to hurt you, I could do it without a giant bottle."

"You could try," Harken said.

I could almost smell the testosterone mixed with a high level of general crankiness. I handed Harken a coffee and suggested that we stop so Iceberg could get a double tub of soda. When they aren't placated with their favorite beverages, humans can be irritable. A moment later, Iceberg sighed as he sipped soda and Harken smiled at the taste of his coffee. My refreshment diplomacy was successful. They might not have achieved absolute harmony, but bitter acrimony had faded some.

We walked in something resembling peace until we reached the heavily fortified Bagel Galleria. Guards with long-range stunners and net launchers stood outside all nineteen bagel shops and kept careful watch of people eating at patio tables. The private security force had been brought in because of recent hostilities between bagel purists and the newest bagel shop in the galleria, Our Bagels Our Way, which insisted on going against the grain and making unconventional bagels. No holes. Soft exterior. Any shape but round. Made with water not imported from the Great American region closest to New York City. "They're basically triangular rolls!" the purists had shouted before rushing into OBOW and throwing chairs at racks of "so-called" bagels. The bagel community was hoping that a unified show of force and solidarity from fellow bagel shops would prevent an escalation of bagel violence. The last thing the bagel industry wanted was to suffer their own version of the Great American Pizza War and its terrible loss of life. No, a free society couldn't let a fringe group of fundamentalist consumers use threats and violence to dictate what was and was not a bagel. Or pizza. Or anything else. If OBOW wanted to make triangular, holeless, soft rolls and pretend they were bagels, as under-standably offensive as it was to people with remotely decent taste and respect for tradition, that was between them and whatever undiscerning customers they managed to attract.

Harken was not in the mood for a bagel, not even a real one. He'd had plenty of gluten already, with a baguette earlier in the day and toast with his scrambled eggs dinner. The bagel shops also served coffee, perfectly acceptable brews to most customers but obviously not to Harken, whose coffee standards had recently become unattainable by any coffeemaker that had ever existed except me. He was drinking the coffee I'd just handed him anyway, and besides, anyone else who foolishly attempted to give him coffee would find themselves on the business end of a vibrational saw.

Past the tense security of the Bagel Galleria and down one level was the utter delight of people lining the parade promenade in Blue Neighborhood 319. It was a perfect day for a parade, like every other day in the Great American. Daily parades never got old because there was always something different to commemorate. Today happened to be the annual Great American Day of older siblings, chicken broth, attached earlobes, butter that wasn't really butter but still tasted pretty good as long as you weren't picky, men under the height of five foot six, shoe store workers,[122] appreciating extinct animals that were no longer extinct, lens games, and handheld tools. Floats celebrating these were led by forty-seven acrobats on stilted pogo sticks backflipping in unison as they juggled small fiery torches. They were accompanied by marching music from 112 high-kicking accordionists in star formation close behind. Above their heads, 1,008 variable-helium balloons bopped up and down in time to the music, precisely synchronized to the accordionists' kicks. Molk lined both sides of the parade route by the thousands and cheered the seventy-seven members of the local coupon battalion, whose digi-rifles zapped discounts directly to customers' lenses. In other words, it was a standard, no-frills Great American parade.

We had left the parade behind and could barely hear the last of the accordions when Nutella showed up out of nowhere and said, "I see you're getting the band back together." As previously established, showing up out of nowhere was her usual method of showing up. That didn't make it any less disconcerting, and Iceberg jumped.[123]

Despite not being named Iceberg, Harken kept his cool and simply greeted Nutella as if she'd walked up to us out in the open like a non-super-secret agent might. "How's it going?"

---

[122] This one was actually celebrated monthly.

[123] It's not clear there was any air between his feet and the floor, so it might be more accurate to say his body made a jump-like motion of surprise.

She was similarly nonplussed.[124] "Not bad. How's your day been?"

"Someone tried to drop a gigantic bottle on my head. Other than that, about the same as usual. Thanks for knocking me clear, by the way. I might be dead if not for you."

"Oh, you'd definitely be dead if not for me. You're welcome. I figured your shiny friend could take the hit for you. Sorry about your hat, Arjay."

Being reminded of my destroyed hat made me sad. It was the best hat I'd ever owned in my entire eight days, and I would miss it forever. "We're not a band," I informed her. "Or a team. Harken and I are partners, but the rest of you are not."

"Thanks for botsplaining," Nutella said.

We reached the expanding crowd waiting to get into the Great American Coliseum. Had I not mentioned we were going to the Coliseum? It's probably something I should have mentioned. Oh, well. That's where we were. Celebrity news reported that's where Sannien had gone shortly after losing his tail, and Harken wanted to talk to Sannien. The entrance façade was a faux stone Coliseum-like archway and columns and large double wood doors.

Harken asked, "What were you doing there? I thought you said even GAD couldn't get into a party like that."

Nutella said, "At the time, I thought we couldn't. We were expecting the party to have top-notch, professional security. Instead, at the last minute, we found out Ten-Toes was handling it and this master of keen observation would be working the door. The party suddenly seemed less impenetrable. Their weapon sniffers are second rate."

Iceberg didn't detect that she was talking about him. He was an executive assistant, not a detective.

Harken asked, "How'd you know Avocado Queen wouldn't be at the party?"

---

[124] Unless where you're from, *nonplussed* means surprised or confused, in which case she was non-non-plussed.

"She told us. Avocado Queen happens to be one of our funders. She told us she was on the guest list and lent me her robe and hat for my disguise."

"Funders?"

"Yes, funders. As in she helps pay for our gear and operating expenses."

"I know what a funder is. I assumed the Great American paid for that, since you defend it and all."

Nutella waved that assumption off. "GAD prefers to remain independent and avoid the bureaucratic entanglements."

"So, if you're not funded by the Great American, who authorizes you to do what you do? You know, the spying, secret missions, hidden bases. Didn't you almost kill someone during our last case?"[125]

"We authorize ourselves."

"I don't think that's how authorizing works. Someone in authority has to approve of your activity, of your existence. Otherwise, you're unauthorized."

"Harken, you're still stuck in an old-fashioned, outside mindset, thinking there's one boss or government in charge of it all. Avocado Queen and others like her have their own motivation to keep the Great American safe. It's part of the system of checks and balances. GAD has always been independently funded and self-authorizing. We do what needs to be done."

They probably would have had a fascinating conversation about the complexities of Great American governance if the doors hadn't opened at that exact moment and the eager, massive crowd all around fighting their way in hadn't shoved us into the Great American Coliseum.

---

[125] I would put a spoiler alert here, but you've either already read *The Great American Deception* and know all about this, or you've taken ignoring my notes to offensive levels and won't see this. Besides, I didn't say whom she almost killed, so this would be a vague spoiler at most, not something that requires an alert unless you're excessively spoiler-phobic, in which case it might be time to seek help for your plot-centricity.

The Coliseum wasn't open air, of course, because in the Great American nothing was. Inside, it didn't resemble the Roman Colosseum[126] at all besides the base of the arena being a similar shape, though the play area of the GAC, as people called the Great American Coliseum, was substantially longer than the ancient Colosseum's 287 feet. The GAC's ovoid, which is like an oval but shaped enough like an egg to deserve a more eggish word, was 400 feet long. The entire area was covered in five levels of generously spaced scaffolding, bright red platforms connected by ramps above and below. Cameras everywhere streamed the action to personal vid screens, and spectators in the bleachers as well as those in their housing units could toggle from scene to scene and watch whichever gladiatorial battles they liked.

Betting was fast and furious. You could wager on anything you could think of. Probably some things you couldn't think of, too. That depends on how imaginative you were. Of course, people bet on who would have the most points and who would be most valuable gladiator, but the side bets were more interesting. Would a jousting player take a foam lance to the groin? Would nearby players laugh? Would one of the laughing nearby players start coughing or choking on their own laughter? Would that cause other nearby players to laugh even harder? Would people argue over whether it was a cough or a choke? Betbots could give you odds on all that and more.

Players formed teams or went solo. Sensors scored hits and damage and displayed totals on leaderboards. There was no flag to capture, no plot or point to the game besides fighting and scoring points so you could move up to the next level and fight some more. This continued until you reached the fifth and final level of the scaffolding and were rewarded with uncomfortable stools and overpriced bars, where even the lowest shelves had top-shelf liquor. Sannien was at that very moment on the fifth

---

[126] They weren't even spelled the same.

level trying to drown his one-tailed sorrows in a bottle from the toppest shelf of all. [127] Unlike ordinary players, influencelebs with sufficient influence already had the points needed to move up all the levels and could go straight to five. Harken, Iceberg, Nutella, and I didn't have that kind of influence, but we were on a case and minutes counted. My partner had no intention of wasting time fake fighting with fake gladiators and wasn't in a gambling mood as we entered level one.

The crowd dispersed, as crowds sometimes do, dozens of people running in all directions to grab ancient hand weapons from racks and put on bulky armor and heavy helmets that made it hard to see. On level one, people pretending to be gladiators wielded foam swords and axes and defended themselves with resin shields. Lifesize whirligigs of spinning lions and dragons and ogres broke up the space between castle forts. A group of gladiators pushed a catapult into position to begin the attack. They were there for a bachelor party and they'd already had a few drinks, which could be why their foam projectile missed the castle by thirty feet. Or maybe they just had bad aim.

Since we weren't trying to earn points, we headed straight for the ramp at the far end to level two. We weren't wearing armor or carrying weapons. That, along with Iceberg's tuxedo, Nutella's mini skirt, Harken's black shirt and pants, and my not being a person at all, should have alerted gladiators that we weren't participating in the game, but a group of four foolishly decided that this lack of gear and appropriate costuming made us an easy target. They charged at us, axes and swords raised, shouting incomprehensibly for maximum intimidation. I almost felt bad for them. How could they know they were attacking perhaps the most skilled combatant in the entire Great American, a secret agent who was never play fighting?

Nutella ran at them. She certainly had weapons on her—she always had a rifle or two hidden somewhere. They wouldn't be necessary. She bounded like a cat—not one of the lazy ones that

---

[127] Unfortunately, this wouldn't work. Sorrows were strong swimmers.

sleep all day—over their heads, flipping and twisting to land close behind them. Before they could turn around to face her, she'd already swept the legs of two of them. They fell hard. In an instant she was back on her feet, wrested the sword from another and kicked the axe out of another another's hands. Nutella wacked the swordless gladiator in the helmet with his own sword and side-kicked the axeless gladiator right in her armored stomach. The four attackers were on the floor, frightened beyond fright because ouch that hurt, and why was this mini skirt warrior playing so mean? They made no attempt to get up or fight back as Nutella tossed the foam sword aside.

We caught up to Nutella and continued toward the ramp. Vid of the scuffle immediately spread among players and spectators. No one else would be charging at us looking for a fight, and quite a few people were now betting on Nutella to seriously injure someone. A broken bone had three-to-one odds. At the ramp were three bouncers checking scores before letting people move up to the next level. They were strong and sturdy, each about the same size as Harken. Like everyone else, they had seen what Nutella could do, and they glanced at the towering Iceberg, whose shoulders were as broad as a castle. The precise educational background of the bouncers was not known, but they weren't titanically stupid, and quickly stepped aside to let us pass.

Level two featured players dressed in monk robes pretending to be copyrighted space wizards and dueling with humming simulated laser swords. The power move they tried again and again was to attack opponents and then claim to be their father. Space wizards were weird. However, space wizards were also wise, and having seen the vid of Nutella taking out four players and noting that Iceberg was as big as an iceberg, they wisely avoided us as we walked to the next ramp, where, for the same reason, the bouncers were as accommodating as at the previous one.

We entered level three and I told Harken my analysis was complete, because it was.

"What analysis?" he asked, as players around us shot each other with high-velocity ping-pong-ball rifles.

"General Major Driver's hair," I said.

"I have no idea what you're talking about," Harken said.

He couldn't hear my response over the pop-pop-pop of ping-pong balls as we walked past machine-gun nests and dozens of small barriers where players took cover. On level three, many wore goggles, heeding the signs that said *It's all fun and games until someone loses an eye.*[128] Others rejected the warning as fake news propaganda, and several had the detached retinas to prove it. The GAC didn't mind if people didn't wear goggles as long as release forms had been completed.

Since Harken had no idea what I was talking about, when we'd cleared the ping-pong war zone and he could hear me again, I told him I'd tested a strand of Driver's hair to find out the composition of the gel he uses.

"You what?"

"Tested his hair."

"How'd you get his hair?"

"I acquired it at the party. It turns out the gel is just standard, nothing you can't buy anywhere."

"Arjay, why are you telling me this? Why should I care about the gel he uses?"

"You shouldn't. I was curious, however, because his hair has a sheen I couldn't quite explain. I assumed it was something exotic in his gel, but now that I've completed my analysis, I know that's not it. The special sheen of his hair isn't from the gel at all, but from being thoroughly washed with pasta water."

"Pasta water?"

"Yes. The starchy water used to cook pasta is full of minerals and vitamins, perfect for keeping hair healthy and giving it a luxurious sheen. Using it instead of shampoo was a popular trend for a while on the outside."

---

[128] Unless you were playing Find the Eye, in which case that's when the fun and games started, according to official rules.

Harken smiled a sudden, broad smile. He already knew all about the benefits of washing hair with pasta water and how popular it had been for a while on the outside. "Great work, Arjay! Now it all makes sense."

"It does?"

"Not all of it. Some of it does, I think. Good work, partner. Maybe we should change your name to *Deus Ex Machina*."

"No, thank you. That's too many syllables. I prefer *Arjay*."

"I don't suppose you happened to check the DNA on that hair as well?"

I had not, but since my partner suggested it, I began DNA analysis as we reached level four, which was devoted to jousting. Simulated legless horses[129] on horizontal tracks allowed players to launch at each other with foam-tipped lances. Dislodged jousters landed on heavy padding. It was generally a safe activity. We passed the decorative windmills and a player curled up on the floor still recovering from taking a lance to his groin, a bet that had paid off two to one for spectators in the bleachers and wagering from home.

We had made it through all four Great American Coliseum combat zones and those in our group who had a respiratory system, unlike me, could breathe a sigh of relief if they wanted to, though they didn't seem to want to. Harken, Iceberg, and Nutella were relaxed about the whole pretend-fighting experience. Ahead, intimidated bouncers stepped aside as we walked up the fourth and final ramp leading to level five, where we found excellent bars and some of the best chairs ever made.

---

[129] Finally, an end to equine erasure! Except for the legs.

After the brilliant inventor Vinci Rapport had built an incomparable legacy of benevolence with his revolutionary product Sock Rapport (which improved life in the Great American in more ways than I can hope to document in this account of our third case), he moved on to a new, deeply personal project: designing the perfect chair. Many people throughout recorded history[130] had worked at improving the design of the common chair. It wasn't something most gave much thought to until they sat in an uncomfortable one. Then they might think, *Chairs have been around almost as long as human backsides. How is it possible uncomfortable chairs still existed?* Yet exist they did. Even in the Great American, some chairs were too soft and some were too firm, some were too high and some were too low, some were comfortable but ugly and others were beautiful but painful to sit in, and some had other drawbacks, like no built-in

---

[130] And a good deal that wasn't recorded and hence wasn't history.

cupholder. Of course, there were also many excellent chairs, but the perfect one had yet to be designed. Changing that became Rapport's new life goal.

He had so far designed and built eighty-two distinct prototype chairs in this noble quest. And as beautiful and luxurious as each was, he eventually found fault with every single one before moving on to designing and building the next. The chairs piled up in his design studio and then the warehouse space he borrowed from his own company, Sock Rapport Unlimited. Pretty soon it became clear he couldn't hold onto every flawed chair. Anyway, he had no use for them—they weren't *the one*. There was no sense letting the chairs go to waste, though, despite their lack of perfection, and he decided to give them to a friend who was starting a new business called the Great American Coliseum (you've probably heard of it). And that's how level five of the GAC ended up with an array of unique, almost-perfect chairs designed by the creative genius inventor Vinci Rapport.

It was these chairs and fine free drinks that attracted celebs. Mostly it was the chairs. Bragging rights came with sitting in a Vinci Rapport original. It was also a good opportunity for self-vids, promoting a new project, talking up a forthcoming appearance at a retail location, selling a trademarked hair style. Plus, the chairs were exceptionally comfortable—some reclined, some had extendable footrests, some had scalp massagers, all had cupholders. Each of these fine sitting apparatuses was on a separate round twelve-foot diameter red platform, elevated like a throne[131] above a bevy of barstools all around.

Beneath each unique chair, each platform had a circular bar protruding from its hollowed-out base and a bartender inside mixing artisanal cocktails for the non-celebs sitting on barstools ten feet below the chaired celebs. The barstools weren't comfortable and the drinks were expensive, but by scoring enough points and making it through all the levels, GAC players

---

[131] If the symbolism feels heavy-handed, let me point out that I didn't design the place.

could hang out uncomfortably and expensively just a few feet below actual famous people, and that's what mattered. It's true that many of the famous people in the chairs were famous mainly for being famous and in a couple of cases famous for being related to someone famous for being famous, but that didn't dampen the enthusiasm of the fans on barstools who had fought through four levels for the privilege of enjoying this very moment.

An intricate network of catwalks[132] connected all the throne platforms so celebs could visit each other without coming into contact with the sweaty faux gladiators below. It also connected them with the much larger center elevated platform where celebs could get massages, manicures, pedicures, and other more delicate personal grooming in enclosed pamper pods. Above it all, across the 400-foot length of the arena and the bleachers full of betting spectators watching the action on all four levels of the Great American Coliseum, the massive domed ceiling displayed a never-ending quick-cut montage of fight scenes and car chases from all the movies ever made.

Sitting on one of the chairs on one of the red platforms was Sannien, and he was more than just drunk. His Great American Inebriation Ranking (GAIR) was 12,922. It was generally agreed that anyone with a GAIR in five figures or lower had consumed far too much alcohol. I didn't understand the human pre-occupation with a beverage that depressed the senses. Perhaps that was because of my bias as a coffeemaker. A drink should lift you up with energy—sure, a good cup might make you talk more quickly than you intend, but that was better than one that made you slur your words. From up on his platform, Sannien's

---

[132] Felines of any kind were not permitted on the catwalks because GAC's owner had bad allergies. Canines of the doodlepoo variety were allowed because the owner wasn't allergic to them and in fact owned three little floofs that he sometimes brought to work. Sadly, I didn't see them on the premises at the moment, but nevertheless, for the sake of clarity, I will henceforth refer to these specific catwalks as *dogwalks*.

shouted words were so slurred they all ran into each other and had become one long word that wasn't easy to understand.

"Iusedtohavetwotailsbutonegotcutoff!" He shout-whined the word(s) again and leaned further back on one of the most comfortable chairs ever designed and built, looking up at the ceiling to see a 1977 black Pontiac Trans Am being chased by a police car.

Crowded all around us, gladiators were drinking and pointing at celebs in the chairs above. Harken said we weren't there to bask in secondhand celeb glory. We were there to get some answers from Sannien. I told Harken it didn't look like Sannien had any answers. His head rolled back and he again shouted, "Iusedtohavetwotailsbutonegotcutoff!" The ceiling showed martial arts legend Bruce Lee fighting a tall basketball player.

"Well," Harken said, "I'm not gonna stand here all day listening to this. Iceberg, give me a boost."

"What?"

"Give me a boost."

"You want me to lift you up?"

"Yes. That's what 'Give me a boost' means. Lift me up so I can grab onto that catwalk."[133]

Iceberg demurred. "You're not exactly a little guy yourself, you know. I could strain my back."

"Strain your back?"

"That's what I said. I'm not a machine. I have a back."

I informed Iceberg that machines can have backs. "They might not have vertebrae and other organic back-like physiology, but if they have fronts, they usually have backs as well. On one of the other hands, if they are bell-shaped and somewhat cylindrical, like I am, they might not have backs *or* fronts."

Harken shook his head at me in that way he had of expressing disapproval by shaking his head. "Are you done?"

"I am."

---

[133] I had not informed Harken that we would be referring to them as dogwalks.

"Good. Any idea how I'm gonna get up there to talk to Sannien?"

"I could bring the dogwalk down to you."

"What the hell's a dogwalk?"

"That's what we're calling the catwalk now."

Harken said, "Bring it down."

"Bring what down?"

"Arjay, I'm not gonna call it a dogwalk. Bring it down."

We were on a case and minutes counted, so I brought it down. It wasn't difficult. My vibrational saw sliced through the support column in seconds, and the dogwalk slumped in the middle twenty-two feet from the platform on which Sannien sat. Three quick tosses with a precision that would have made The Juggler envious, and my vibrational saw severed the dogwalk completely and it came down a few feet toward us. The other end was still anchored to Sannien's platform, the metal twisted but holding.

Harken asked Nutella and Iceberg to help him pull the loose end to the floor, or would that strain Iceberg's back too much? Iceberg made a face at Harken that clearly conveyed, *No, it won't strain my back too much, but how unpleasant of you to be sarcastic about it.* Working together, the three of them brought the loose end of the dogwalk to the floor and made it a ramp to the platform where Sannien sat, still drunk, whining, and looking at the ceiling, which now showed two chiseled boxers in a ring fighting to determine which superpower nation would win the Cold War.

I was first up the ramp, to make sure it was secure and stable. It was.[134] I didn't have to do any welding or reinforcing when I reached the platform. The metal at the top had twisted but held, as I already mentioned. Harken followed. Iceberg and Nutella stayed below because it wasn't a very large platform and the stupendous chair took up a lot of space. Maybe the lack of

---

[134] Physically, anyway. The emotional toll would not be known until much later, if the ramp turned out to be sentient and have emotions at all, which was unlikely, so this is a note you probably don't need to bother with.

space is why bouncers didn't rush up the makeshift ramp to stop us from bothering Sannien. Or maybe they thought Nutella would kick them in the head if they got too close. Or maybe they'd seen me tossing a vibrational saw. Whatever the reason, no one interfered. Fans had gathered around the bottom of our ramp and closer to the platform so they could be part of the excitement.

Sannien was entranced by the ceiling movie fistfight that went on forever as a man tried to force another man to put on sunglasses. Harken had no interest in the fight, wasn't a science fiction film buff, and waved his hand over Sannien's face to get his attention. The influenceleb's head lolled left and then down. He was still conscious, technically, as this time he mumbled, "Iusedtohavetwotailsbutonegotcutoff!"

"Arjay, give him some coffee to sober him up."

"Frank Harken, as extraordinary as my coffee is, it can't do that."

"What are you talking about? So far today, your coffee's knocked out two sport-coat thugs and healed my arm."

"Yes, my special brews can be quite special, but there are limits. It's a well-known factoid that if you give a drunk coffee, you end up with a wide-awake drunk, not a sober one."

"I'll settle for a wide-awake drunk."

I handed Harken an extra-stimulating brew. He brought the cup to Sannien's lips and held his head steady, assuring our famous friend that a few sips of this delightful beverage would make him feel better about his tail. I won't say anything about the composition of this particular brew except it should not be allowed anywhere near an open flame.

Sannien was now wide-awake. Still drunk, but awake at full width. Were his hands shaking a little? Or a lot? Possibly. And so what if they were? It isn't like he was juggling mini vibe saws. "What the hell!" he said more than asked. "Hey, you're not supposed to be up here!" His words were still slurred but now also full of energy.

Harken spoke calmly and applied just enough pressure to Sannien's neck to let him know that things could become less calm in a hurry if he didn't cooperate. "We're not staying long. Just tell us exactly what the blackmailer said and we'll get out of your hair."[135]

Besides being wide-awake and drunk, Sannien was confused. "Blackmailer?"

"Yes, blackmailer—the message you got saying if unspecified demands were not met, unspecified information would be exposed. What exactly did the message say?"

"I don't know what you're talkin' about."

"Yesterday, did you receive a threatening message?"

"Where's my tail? I think I'm gonna be sick."

"You can throw up when you're done answering my questions."

"I didn't get any damn message about blackmail. What the hell are you talkin' about?"[136]

"General Major Driver said you did."

The coffee really kicked in, and that, mixed with exceptional drunkenness, slurred Sannien's speech in new and interesting ways. If I told you what he actually said, you wouldn't understand it, and neither did Harken. I had to interpret for him. It translated to something like, "Now I understand why you're confused. Driver must've meant *he* got the message. I only receive messages from approved contacts. Anyone else trying to reach me is automatically redirected to him. He's my manager, after all."

"And your approved contacts, would they happen to include Margoria Magnificent?"

No, I translated, they would happen to not. Messages from exes went to Sannien's manager. There were quite a few exes.

"So, you never got any of the pics she sent you?"

---

[135] Fortunately, this is just an expression and we weren't actually in Sannien's hair. Getting out might have been especially difficult given the quantity of sculpting gel needed to keep the front coiffed top in his trademarked style.

[136] He might have used words other than *damn* and *hell*. It was hard to tell with his rapid, slurred speech.

Drunk as he was, Sannien snapped to extra wide-awake attention when he heard Margoria had sent him pics. "What pics?" Then the stimulating sips of special coffee wore off and he passed out, slumping in the luxurious chair.

We could have stimulated him some more—besides coffee, I had an electric prod—but Harken said he'd already heard enough. He'd suspected we were being played. Now he knew we were.

When we were out of the Great American Coliseum and walking in Green Neighborhood 210, Harken asked Nutella, "What gives?"

"What gives what?"

"Let's not play games. You know more than you're letting on. I was up on that platform with my hands practically at Sannien's throat and you didn't say a word. Yet earlier today you made a big deal about any threat to his safety being a threat to the entire Great American. Morale or something."

"Oh, that."

"You didn't really expect me to believe GAD's top agent thought Great American security could be undermined by anything happening to that two-tailed punk? So why'd you really want to get into that party? You said there would be an attempted murder, and there was. But that bottle didn't fall on any of those big celebs you were worried about, just me."

"*Almost* fell on you," she said. "You're welcome."

"Nutella..."

"Fine, Harken, you caught me. I thought you might be in danger. The threatening chatter we'd intercepted specifically mentioned you. That's why I wanted Arjay to be on high alert."

"That doesn't make any sense. If you wanted to keep me from danger, why not tell me and Arjay that I was the intended victim? Why the vague warning?"

"If I told you someone was going to try to kill you at the party, would you have attended?"

"I'm not sure. Maybe not."

"There you have it. You don't go to the party, and the bottle doesn't almost drop on you, and the killer is free to make another attempt on your life at some other, unexpected time, when we're not ready for it, some time I might not be around to save you. You don't go to the party, and you wouldn't have found the piece of Margoria's dress. We'd have no clues at all about who wanted you dead. Letting you go to the party was a risk I had to take."

"Let me get this straight. In order to catch the person trying to kill me, you were willing to risk my being killed?"

"Yes," she said.

"Did it work? You don't happen to know who tried to kill me, or why, do you?"

"No, I don't." Just then she got an urgent notification, a shocking bit of news that demanded our complete attention. She couldn't believe it, but her believing it was not relevant to it being true. "I've never heard of this happening so fast before—Margoria's trial is about to start."

Harken looked at his broken watch. "What? GAS just took her an hour ago. They're having a trial tonight? Has she even had a chance to meet with defense lawyers?"

"Someone's sure in a hurry," Nutella said.

The food court was a short walk away, and the two of them managed to sort out some of the day's events before we reached it. GAD hadn't really intercepted chatter, but had been notified through an anonymous, untraceable message that Harken would be killed at the party. Nutella didn't know who sent the message, because that's what anonymous and untraceable mean. At first Nutella wasn't sure she should trust the message. It could be a hoax, but what would anyone gain by making GAD erroneously think Harken would be killed? Nutella couldn't think of any motive and treated the threat as real.

She immediately bugged Sannien's manager to find out all she could about the party and put me and Harken on alert for possible violence, though she wasn't specific about the threat because, as she previously explained, that might deter us from going to the party in the first place—Nutella believed there was no time like the present and the best way to solve a problem was to confront it. Once she'd alerted us, what she really needed to do was figure out how to get into the party herself. Eavesdropping on Driver paid off later in the morning when he was talking to Ten-Toes about Sannien's upcoming promotion of The Outside Experience. Nutella concluded that Ten-Toes would not tolerate a threat to his marketing plan's safety, and she was the one who made sure the grapevine told him Sannien would be killed at the party. Nutella had pulled strings like a virtuoso. As a result of the threat, Ten-Toes insisted that his crew handle security at Sannien's party, putting Iceberg and sport-coats at the entrance instead of the professional crew that was supposed to handle it, and that, as she'd mentioned earlier, allowed Nutella to evade their weapon sniffers and infiltrate the party disguised as Avocado Queen. [137] Then it was a simple matter of waiting for the killer to make a move. When the giganticest bottle started to topple on Harken and she saw I was paralyzed, Nutella was in position to do what she does best, which is whatever needs to be done. She kept him from being killed and gave us the chance to learn that whoever was behind the attempted murder also wanted Margoria to take the blame.

Harken was impressed. "You had a busy day. Maybe we should change *your* name to *Deus Ex Machina*."[138]

"Very funny, Harken. Don't give me too much credit. Yeah, I worked hard to be in the right place at the right time to save your bacon,[139] but I still have no idea who tried to kill you, why they framed Margoria—if you're right she's being framed—or how they managed to paralyze Arjay at the exact moment the bottle fell. Do you?"

---

[137] Iceberg was walking with us and this time he almost noticed she was talking about him before not noticing at all.

[138] Unacceptable! He'd already offered that name to me!

[139] Between Al the griddle pan's pancakes, Harken's eggs and toast for dinner, and Nutella's saving of bacon, there sure had been a lot of breakfast food today. Plus, plenty of coffee.

"I have some idea about some of it," he said. "That bit you heard Arjay tell me at the Coliseum, about Driver's hair, reminds me of someone I used to know on the outside, someone with a grudge. And I think I now know why Margoria was framed. Anyway, I need more than an idea. I need evidence. We've been so busy reacting to events, we've hardly had a chance to look. We should be looking right now. Instead, we're stuck at a trial, at the mercy of Great American justice."

17

The trial was already underway when we arrived at the food court. Late as it was, 1,083 jurors sat at tables and enjoyed snacks and second desserts (in some cases, third) while listening to testimony from experts. Pirouetting dancers finished spinning and cleared the way for the next witness. The judge sat high behind the lectern and with a waving conductor's baton ensured the trial went smoothly. Margoria Magnificent sat in the Accused Box. Annie was not there. Maybe the dummy was not considered an accomplice, on account of being made of wood and not having a brain.

The prosecutor thanked the peacegrid vid analyst for confirming that the thirty-six viewpoints of the falling gigantic cologne/perfume bottle were not altered in any way, proving beyond any doubt[140] that it was the cause of the shard that sliced through the tail of the famous influenceleb Sannien.

---

[140] Including reasonable and a shadow of.

181

Seven more vids clearly showed the piece of blue fabric caught in the mechanism that had brought down the bottle, and now a dancer executed a graceful, athletic grand jeté as the prosecutor welcomed a textilephile to the witness stand. The expert confirmed that the fabric lodged in the cutting mechanism found inside the bottle's base in fact exactly matched the dress the suspect was known for wearing when she performed her little ventriloquist act.

Other experts were called up. Don't worry! The dancers always completed their moves and stepped to the side before testimony began and no witnesses were accidentally kicked in the throat by a flying pointe—the judge excelled at food court trial choreography.

An eminent celebritologist presented data demonstrating Sannien's popularity with the four most desirable retail demographics. Detailed breakdowns in pie charts and bar graphs showed how dramatically that popularity had skyrocketed upon his acquisition of a second tail. All the marketing metrics increased by double digits, which the celebritologist said was the most digits by which they could increase. There were impressed *oohs* and *ahhs* from dining jurors.

A certified mood optimizer was brought in to attest to the detrimental emotional and physical impact Sannien's lost tail was having on teenagers across the Great American. She didn't use the word *impact* figuratively, she said. The vid of Sannien's tail being sliced off was an act of literal violence against his tens of thousands of devoted fans, who were assaulted every time it came across their visual feed. Though only a couple of hours had passed since the tragic event, several peer-reviewed studies had already determined that the next generation of Great Americans might never recover from the loss of Sannien's tail. Five people gave victim impact statements along with a list of medications they had started taking.

The whole time, Margoria sat quietly. She hadn't looked away from the judge and witnesses until the fifth victim finished testifying. That's when she saw Harken, who was standing with me near a cluster of tables twenty-eight feet from the Accused

Box. I won't say she suddenly had hope in her eyes because what would that look like? Instead, I'll say she had hope on her face, evidenced by a slight relaxation of the jaw, and her torso, which eased a little as she let out a breath she'd been holding too long. Harken seemed to want to give her a reassuring gesture but didn't know any.

The judge conducted four dancers through a brief kick-line and spoke when they'd stepped aside. "Does the prosecution rest?" she asked.

The prosecutor responded yes, and it was true. He lowered his head into his folded arms on the table where he sat and closed his eyes. Working at night food court was tiring and there wasn't anything left for him to say. The evidence hadn't spoken for itself, because if it did he wouldn't have been needed at all, but the evidence had nonetheless been utterly convincing.

Night food court defense was not always the best defense. The lawyer who was supposed to be on duty had called in sick at the last minute, something about blowing out a kneecap in a homemade pickling accident. The only available replacement had worked the food court all day, a full docket of cases. Also, before being told he had to pull an overnight shift, he'd eaten a large helping of triple-tryptophan turkey for late dinner with a glass of wine and taken an antihistamine because of his allergy to the five doodlepoos who lived with him in his level-five housing unit. Which is to say that the lawyer for the defense was leaning back in his seat, fast asleep and lightly snoring.

Since the defense was also resting, the judge was ready to move on to the deliberating portion of the trial, when dining jurors would vote on the matter of The Great American v. Margoria Magnificent. Two-thirds of the jury voting guilty was needed to convict. Was the jury ready to make its decision?

Iceberg had drifted off somewhere to get a double tub of soda. Nutella, in that secretive way she had of disappearing whenever legal authorities were present, had disappeared.

Harken stepped forward. "I object!" he said, loud enough to be heard throughout the food court.

Dining jurors gasped.

The judge was flabbergasted, the most shocked kind of gasted possible. "You can't object," she said.

"I just did," he said.

Jurors gasped again.

"Who are you?"

I answered for him. "Your Majestic Judgeship, this is Detective Frank Harken."

"That's right, Your Honor. I'm Frank Harken. I've been working this Sannien tail case all night."

The judge frowned. "You have no standing here, detective."

I pointed out that the judge was incorrect. "He isn't seated, Your Gloriousness."

She used that annoyed voice people in authority use when they're annoyed. "Pipe down there, little appliance."

I wasn't a pipe, nor was I little for my size. I was about to say so, but Harken patted my not-head to silence me. I didn't prefer to have my not-head patted, though in deference to my partner's greater experience in matters of the law, I kept quiet.

"Your Honor, Sannien is my client. I am speaking as his investigative representative. Also, I might point out that while the shard sliced his tail, it was my head the bottle almost fell on. I was the one almost killed at the party. That should count for something."

"Detective Harken, you are a fairly well-known personage, perhaps considered famous in some limited circles, but Sannien is a major influenceleb, with fans from coast to coast. There's really no comparison."

Now some jurors laughed.

"I don't really think that's—" he started to say, but the judge wasn't done.

"—Detective Harken, since you insist on talking when you should be listening, let me remind you that if your appliance there hadn't interfered with the falling bottle, it would not have shattered the way it did and a shard would not have flown across the room and severed Sannien's tail. Following the Transference Principle of Guilt that makes owners responsible for the actions of their devices, you could be considered an accessory to the aggravated assault."

Jurors hooted. Someone blasted an airhorn.

Harken worked hard to respond to the judge in a calm, measured voice. "You're saying I could be charged for not being crushed to death by a gigantic falling bottle?"

"Precisely," the judge said.

"If it comes to that, fine. What I want to know is why this trial is being fast-tracked. The Happy Birthday Killer had a week to prepare a defense. How come Margoria gets an hour?"

"Detective, you're not a lawyer. If you had proper legal training, you'd know that justice delayed is justice denied. This food court is committed to expeditiously protecting victims of violence."

"Does it matter at all to this food court that Margoria Magnificent had nothing to do with making that bottle fall?"

"You have evidence to prove this?"

"For one, Margoria had no motive. Why would she drop a bottle on me?"

"She isn't being charged with dropping a bottle on you. She's being charged with slicing off Sannien's tail. You know very well that she had a motive for that. It's called jealousy. Maybe you've heard the saying about a scorned woman. It's from an old poem."

Harken didn't give up. "Besides motive, there's logic. How could Margoria have known that dropping a bottle on me would result in Sannien's tail being sliced off? She couldn't have. You said yourself that if not for my appliance, the bottle wouldn't have shattered the way it did and the shard would not have flown across the room and severed Sannien's tail. The odds of it happening are astronomical."

The judge disagreed. "I said evidence, not logic. This is a legal proceeding, not philosophy class. And the odds of it happening are 100%, since that's exactly what happened. The evidence is clear. Her dress snagged inside the bottle when she was setting up the mechanism that made the bottle fall and deprived Sannien and his fans of a second tail. Cause and effect."

As jurors cheered the judge for such devastating summation, Harken refrained from shaking his head, pressed on. "How do you know it was her dress? Someone else could have been wearing the same dress. Someone could have planted the fabric there to implicate her. I believe that is exactly what happened."

"You're grasping at straws now. Have you ever heard of Occam's razor?[141] *Someone else could have.* Well, yes, I suppose someone else could have waved a magic wand and caused the bottle to fall. This is a food court of law and the jury will consider the evidence, not fantasyland stories. Do you have evidence of fabric being planted? No? I didn't think so. The jury has seen the vid, heard the testimony of the experts, and they know that the accused fled when GAS came looking for her. Everyone knows innocent people don't run from authorities. Innocent people have no reason to fear the law. You have wasted enough of our time here. Now the jury will vote."

Based on the look on his face, Harken might have been having a brief vision of a scene from an ancient movie, a man shouting "It's a madhouse! A madhouse!" while being sprayed by a powerful hose held by a talking gorilla. Harken didn't shout that. He didn't shout anything at all as the jury voted.

The instantaneous result was no surprise to anyone yet completely surprised Harken. He expected the jury to convict since juries love to convict. It's basically their job, he told me. However, he hadn't expected them to convict with prejudice. But that's exactly what they did. Margoria wasn't just guilty. She was extra guilty. He realized this verdict was about more than Sannien. It was a message to everyone in the Great American that attacks on celebrities would not be tolerated.

---

[141] Named for William of Ockham, a clean-shaven philosopher and theologian whose wide-ranging life's work was often reduced to the popular contemporary belief that only the most obvious explanation is always correct.

The extra-guilty verdict enabled the judge to make an example of Margoria. The violent ventriloquist would pay no restitution, wouldn't be banned from shopping retail, wouldn't even be given the option of adrenosnooze implantation. No, for the crime of slicing off Sannien's tail with prejudice, Margoria Magnificent was sentenced to exile. The accused and now convicted young woman screamed, "No!" before guards led her away.

Harken stood silently while all around him jurors high-fived and gamblers checked if their winnings had been deposited yet. The judge declared a recess and dancers took the floor.

Iceberg lumbered back with his double tub of soda and a roasted emu drumstick, which in his humongous hand seemed no larger than a piece of chicken. "Did I miss anything?"

Harken ignored him and headed in the direction the guards had taken Margoria, through the back of the food court to a holding cell. I accompanied him, of course, because I always do. Iceberg trailed behind us, slowly, his attention on his food and drink to prevent any spills on his white tuxedo. Don't worry! It was made of the most advanced stain-repelling fabric and any liquid that touched it would bead up and fall away.[142]

Now that Margoria was being exiled, she had her own holding cell. Two guards scanned Harken for weapons and told him to stand on the yellow line ten feet away. He had five minutes.

Margoria's face was drawn. She'd been crying. She sat on a long bench attached to the rear wall of the cell, her arms wrapped around her knees, which were pulled up almost to her chin. "I thought you were going to get me out of here."

"So did I."

"You promised."

---

[142] The textilephile expert from the trial could probably tell you more about it.

Harken might have argued that she'd pressured him into promising, but he knew it made no difference either way. She was right. He'd promised. And they were going to exile her. "I'm sorry."

"What happens now?"

"They'll give you three days of food and water and retrieve personal items you request from your housing unit."

"Will they let me bring Annie?"

"If you want."

"I do. And after I have Annie and my things, what then?"

"Then you'll leave through an approved exit with as much as you can take with you."

"What's it like outside?"

Harken hesitated. "Depends where outside you are. There are two approved exits in this region. One's in an independent zone. Rural, not at war, recovering. Good water supply, has reliable electricity now from what I hear. Do you have any experience out in the country?"

"Only at the Treeseeum. I've lived my entire life in the Great American. Do you think people there might need a ventriloquist?"

"A ventriloquist? Um, anything's possible. I'm sure people in rural areas appreciate good entertainment, like anyone else. Doubt it's any way to make a living, though."

"What's at the other exit?"

"It's not too far from Denver. Mostly government-controlled. More people there, better infrastructure, could be some opportunities. Your experience cooking tapas might be in some demand—there are wealthier sections, restaurants. But there's still active fighting from time to time. Copbots strictly enforce curfew. You'll need to be careful."

"I don't want to go."

"I know."

"This is your fault."

It didn't matter if it was or wasn't. They were going to exile her. Harken didn't respond. Maybe he half-shrugged, like he was trying to shake something off.

"Isn't there anything you can do?"

"I don't know. I don't want to give you false hope. We still have a few hours while they process the paperwork.[143] I'll do my best."

Harken's time was up. The guards stepped between them.

Iceberg had finished his emu leg and soda and needed just a minute to visit the bathroom. Harken told him to take his time. As soon as the big man was out of sight, we left.

"Won't Iceberg be upset with us for leaving him behind?"

Harken said he didn't care if he was.

"Are we going to break Margoria Magnificent out of her holding cell? My vibrational saw would cut through those bars in 14.7 seconds. The two guards wouldn't be able to stop me."

"No, we're not breaking Margoria out. What are we going to do after that, fight off the entire Great American?"

"I suppose that would be difficult."

"Yes, it would. Don't bother calculating the odds."[144]

"At least the second outside exit doesn't sound too bad, aside from the curfew. Maybe Margoria could get a good job performing with Annie at daytime parties if no restaurants are hiring."

"I don't think she'd last forty-eight hours out there."

"Oh. You didn't tell her that."

"No," Harken said. "I didn't."

He was quiet for a few minutes as we walked and his detective brain deduced away. I didn't distract him by talking. In the past eight days, I'd learned that it was sometimes best to let him think—yes, despite not being a person, I was capable of personal growth.

Periwinkle Neighborhood 203 was below throng density this late at night. People still shopped for shoes, of course, and

---

[143] Even when there was no paper, there was always paperwork.

[144] It was too late, of course. But I kept the unpropitious numbers to myself.

we had to weave through crowds near popular mini-golf courses, especially renaissance paintings and the horror golf attraction Land of Peanuts. A few globe heads still stumbled around behind guidebots, but many molk [145] had long since headed to bed, their day done. Not us. It might have seemed that the case was over, that judgment had been passed, that all hope was lost, but Harken and Arjay[146] weren't done yet. Up ahead, beyond a candy shop and a jewelry store, was a bank of elevators for the residential district. My partner let out a sigh as we got in the elevator. I handed him a coffee.

---

[145] I haven't been using this word much, since some do find it offensive, but at the time of these events, it was still common parlance.

[146] That was me. I don't normally refer to myself in the third person, partly because I'm not a person, but it has a certain dramatic flair, don't you think?

190

18

Matching hair DNA to the correct origin database took longer than expected. I'd been running tracking protocols in the background ever since our visit to the Great American Coliseum. I had to navigate firewalls, security clearances, and deliberately misleading trails. Some of the firewalls had their own firewalls. Driver clearly didn't want people to connect him to his outside past. When I finally had confirmation, we were already on level fourteen of the residential district.

"Won't General Major Driver be sleeping by now?"

Maybe, Harken said. Or he might be awake, expecting us. It didn't matter either way. We'd wake him from a coma if we had to.

The doors slowly glided by on either side of the corridor as we walked. Level fourteen was the second highest and therefore second most expensive and luxurious residential level, and it showed. Even in the corridor outside the housing units, the carpet was pristine and lush.[147] The sconce lighting at the landing moving along with Driver's unit was cheery and bright, bringing out the shininess of shiny authentic fake military medals mounted on the door. Harken knocked. No answer. He didn't knock a second time. He knew that minutes still counted. "Open it."

Opening it was easy. Vibrational saws are more powerful than housing unit doors. Inside was dark until I told the lights to come on and then we could see that just about everything was gold-plated, including walls and shelves displaying many industry plaques and trophies for being the best manager of famous people, or in the top ten at least. There were more medals hanging here and there and other places. In elaborate gold frames, holo-pics of the General Major with celebs filled the gaps. A pic with Name at an exhibit of some of his most well-known art. A pic with John Johnjohnson at a conference of important business executives. A pic with Sannien, both tails visible, at the gala opening of the latest Win-Fall location. A pic with The Juggler in front of the Pentagon. In every pic, the General Major's hair looked fantastic.

The layout resembled other level fourteen units that featured an open-concept design. A large central living space had a gourmet kitchen, fourteen-seat dining table, two wrap-around sofas, three 200-inch wall-embedded screens, full-size playglobe on a pedestal, grand piano, and a hallway leading to the den, bedrooms, bathrooms, and personal hygiene evaporator pods. Harken handed me his half-full coffee and went to inspect the other rooms. I stayed in the central living space and admired the medals on the walls.

Harken returned, checked under the sofas, opened kitchen cabinets, made sure the piano was a real piano that had innards

---

[147] Not quite as lush as the corridor carpet on level fifteen, which, as I indicated in my account of our first case, I can't do full justice to with words due to the shortness of the human lifespan. Level-fourteen carpet would take less time to describe, but still more than we had available, since Harken was walking at a pace that indicated minutes counted.

and wasn't a hollowed-out hiding space. I looked in the refrigerator and was saddened to learn that it was incapable of even rudimentary communication, had no capacity to observe, and would be unable to provide any clues. It was not my favorite refrigerator. "I don't detect General Major Driver anywhere."

Harken asked, "What about in the playglobe?"

"I can't tell. Too much interference from all its tech."

He walked over to the seven-foot sphere and pressed a couple of buttons, engaging the centrifugal drive. "I'm not an expert at these things, but I do know how to turn on the spin cycle."

The playglobe started to spin on its pedestal, slowly at first and then not slowly and then pretty fast and then too fast to be good for anyone who might be inside and then a little faster than that. After a minute and forty seconds, the centrifugal drive disengaged and the sphere began to stop spinning. The interference from the playglobe's tech had kept me from sensing the subtle vital signs within, but after spinning at a-little-faster-than-too-fast speed, the signs were no longer subtle.

"Either this playglobe has a heart," I said, "Or someone inside is in distress."

"Come out, Driver."

The person in the playglobe didn't answer.

"Come out, or we do the spin cycle again."

The door silently hissed as it slid open from bottom to top, and General Major Driver stumbled out. Instead of its usual white pastiness, his face was a shade of green that suggested vomiting might occur. It would be a shame if he got sick, since he was still wearing his crisp uniform festooned with medals. I wondered if he ever took it off. Sleeping in uniform probably had its advantages. You were already dressed for the occasion if a war happened to break out in your bedroom.

Harken took Driver by the elbow and helped him to a seat on one of the sofas. His face was soon a less nauseous shade of green. He breathed deeply and shook his head to fight off the dizziness. His fantastic, smooth hair barely moved.

"We don't have all day," Harken said. "You can confess now."

Driver had just about regained his senses. "Confess? I don't know what you're talking about."

"I said we don't have all day. You have one chance to tell me the truth or we do this the hard way." Harken didn't specify what the hard way would entail.

Driver started to say, "I don't know what—" but was interrupted by a thunderclap slap to the side of his face that nearly knocked him off the sofa.

"Maybe you didn't hear me, General Major. I said we don't have all day."

Driver struggled to sit back up. A handprint on his face was already beginning to swell. He stammered, "I'm your client. You work for me. You have no right—"

"—I have no right? I have no right? You told me Sannien received a blackmail message. I know that's a lie. If anyone received the message, it was you. But there was no message, was there? There never was a blackmail. You told me that to get me to come to the party. Where someone tried to kill me."

Driver was silent.

"I know why you framed Margoria. She was sending Sannien pics, pics Sannien didn't get because they came to you. These were the kind of pics that might get Sannien's attention. That's why you didn't tell him about them. If Margoria got through to him, got his attention, it might end his thing with The Juggler, or threaten it, anyway. You couldn't risk that."

Driver might have been about to say he didn't know what Harken was talking about, stopped himself. His cottage-cheese-textured cheek was red and swollen.

Harken didn't hit him again. He was too busy explaining the motive. "He's quite a talent. The Pentagon isn't a bad venue for a newcomer, but that's just a start. It's small-time for someone as extraordinary as The Juggler. You know he's gonna be big, bigger than Sannien one day. Gonna make you enough money to move to level fifteen and cover the walls there with fake medals. Sannien promoting him makes one day come that much sooner. You'd like to keep them together as long as possible. Even if he and Sannien break it off eventually, you can probably still manage them both if it's amicable. But if a break-up is ugly, if Sannien dumps him for an ex like Margoria, embarrasses him, maybe you lose one of them. Maybe you lose both if you play it wrong. Getting Margoria out of the picture makes that less likely. You can keep two stars. Do I have it right, more or less?"

Driver didn't answer.

"I've thought for a while today there might not have been a blackmail at all. You could have worked a little harder on that setup. Did you even workshop your story? Anonymous blackmailer, no demands—it's just lazy. I had my doubts from the beginning. But the Great American's a strange place. Anything's possible. So I went along, kept my eyes out for suspects. I entertained the possibility there really was a blackmail and a blackmailer. Everything I found told me you can't blackmail Sannien, it's just not possible. He's an open book—the pages are empty, but the book's open.[148] He's incapable of feeling shame. The worse he acts, the more popular he gets. If he did something horrible and word got out, he'd probably gain a million more followers. And that's why you wouldn't be bothered in the first place if someone blackmailed him—in his business, any publicity is good publicity.

"But while I thought there might not be a blackmail, I didn't *know*, not for sure. For that I needed to talk to Margoria and Sannien to learn about the pics. Then it all came together. Well, not all of it. I knew it was you who'd framed Margoria and knew why—you had a motive. It was greed, plain and simple. You've tried to ruin her life, all for a little money."

Driver said, "I admit none of this, but if you've seen The Juggler's act, then you know it was for *a lot* of money. You said yourself he's going to be big, bigger than Sannien."

---

[148] I told you Harken sometimes fell into making old-timey references. A *book* was a collection of paper pages glued together that people used to pretend to have read.

"Greed I could understand. People treating fellow human beings like trash to make some money, that wasn't anything new. What took a while to figure out was why someone wanted to kill me. Why *you* wanted to kill me. You were the one who'd lured me to the party where a bottle almost crushed me. What reason could you possibly have? I'd never even heard of General Major Driver until this morning, why should he want me dead? But then, this is the Great American, and some people change their names, some people come in from the outside and start over, or think they can. Isn't that right, Sergeant Benedict? Or should I call you the Rigatoni Bandit?"

"I don't know what you're talking about."

"Sure you don't. The altered face, the manager persona and successful career, the absurd uniform—I didn't spot any resemblance at all."

"I never heard of any rigatoni thief."

I helpfully corrected him. "It's *bandit*, not thief."

"Arjay, what do I always say about coincidences?"

"That you're not a big believer in them."

"Right. So, when someone tries to kill me, and that someone happens to use pasta water as shampoo, a rare thing in the Great American, it's gonna make me remember that ten years earlier, I busted someone for stealing tons of rigatoni and using it to sell black market pasta-water shampoo. And am I gonna think it's a coincidence?"

"No," I said. "No, you are not."

Driver mustered some gumption and shouted, "I'm a respected member of the celebrity-management community! I don't have to sit here and listen to this!"

"We've [149] already run DNA analysis, Benedict. We know exactly who you are. You're the same ex-cop I put away for being the Rigatoni Bandit. What I don't understand is why now? You've been in the Great American for seven years. I've been here a couple, long enough that any burning desire you had for

---

[149] This was more *me* than *we*, but since we were a team, I let Harken share the credit.

vengeance should have pushed you to come after me before today. So why now? Why risk this successful career you've built?"

"I don't know what you're talking about."

"You're still gonna play that game? We have receipts. We know who you are."

"Detective, there is no law against changing my name. Like you said, people do it all the time in here. There's no law against starting over in the Great American. Whatever identity I had out there doesn't matter."

"I know you framed Margoria. You made that bottle fall."

"Do you have any evidence? Because the court already saw evidence that proves Margoria was behind it. She's already been convicted."

"Evidence? You're the damn Rigatoni Bandit! You have motive."

"Motive, shmotive. That's you being imaginative, melodramatic. You have no evidence. I had nothing to do with the bottle falling on you. You say there's no blackmailer, I say I received a message from a blackmailer. You misheard me, or maybe I misspoke. The message came to me, not Sannien. But it was anonymous, untraceable, poof, it disappeared. I hired you in good faith this morning. Margoria tried to kill Sannien in a fit of jealous rage but missed and almost killed you. She's not well in the head, that one."

Harken seemed to be considering another thunderclap slap but controlled himself. "Benedict, here's what's going to happen. First, you're gonna tell me who you're working with, how you were able to paralyze Arjay when the bottle fell."

"I don't know what you're talking about. And don't misname me. I'm General Major Driver."

"You're gonna tell me. Then we're going to the food court and you're gonna tell the judge you put that fabric in the bottle to frame Margoria. You're gonna tell the truth."

Driver shook his head. "That's not happening."

"You still wanna do this the hard way, huh?"

"Detective, I'm not a fighter, not anymore." In his awkward position on the sofa, he tried to straighten his military uniform. "I haven't seen action in a long time, not since my career in law enforcement ended, but you know all about that. You can hit me again. Beat me all night. There is no way I'm turning myself in to a food court. I'm innocent. Force me to say I did it and I'll show them this bruise on my face, the door you destroyed breaking into my housing unit to coerce me. I'm a respected member of the community. I manage the third most famous influenceleb in the entire Great American. There's no evidence I did anything at all. You know that's true. You're lucky if I don't call GAS about this assault."

Harken raised his fist, thought hard about punching Driver in the face. Instead, he turned, started toward the door, and said, "We're not done, you and I."

"And Frankie, I hope you've learned something about loyalty today. You can't just betray the blue wall and get away with it."

Harken stopped midstride, clenched his fist.

Driver said, "Go on, Frankie, get out of here. Margoria's being exiled and it's completely your fault. You reap what you sow, Fraaankieee, Fraaaankieeee, Fraaaankieeee..."

Harken was silent and still for twelve seconds, a long time to be silent and still. He never turned around to look at Driver. Then he walked out.

The taunting, "Fraaankieee, Fraaankieee, Fraaankieee..." followed us as we left the housing unit and headed out of the residential district. Harken didn't look back. The night was not over yet. Minutes still counted.

Frank[150] Harken didn't want to admit it, but General Major Driver Sergeant Benedict Rigatoni Bandit was right. DNA might prove who he was, but that wouldn't mean anything to a Great American food court. Who he was didn't matter. He was allowed to change his name, leave his past behind. It was part of what made the Great American so attractive to outsiders.[151] Humans liked to believe they could move somewhere and start over, as if becoming a new person were as simple as changing scenery and taking on a different name. It was the Great American way. Despite not changing his name, even Ten-Toes had a fresh start after coming in from the outside.

Driver's *real identity*, if that term still had any meaning, didn't prove anything. Pasta-water hair wasn't enough. What we needed was evidence tying him to the falling bottle that almost

---

[150] His name was not *Frankie*. I suggest you avoid calling him that.

[151] In addition to mini-golf.

killed Harken and severed Sannien's tail. That's what we were looking for on the garden level, the manufacturing district beneath the Great American. Staffed entirely by specialized bots that worked around the clock,[152] the large and small factories and shops were a hive of constant activity. (Please don't be confused—*hive* is metaphorical; they were bots, not insects.) However, the hallways with their white cinderblock walls that seemed to go forever were a hive of constant inactivity. People didn't bother coming down here very much. It was just us walking this way and that, passing viewing windows of bots making shoes, mini playglobes, massive vid screens, tiny ear speakers, and glowing nail polish (and other things). It was easy enough to determine where the giant bottle of Sannien's Smell had been manufactured. Production transparency was an early Great American principle, with many companies even allowing tour groups onto factory floors to watch products being made up close, an activity that had been fairly popular until it wasn't.

The bottle had been assembled in a small fabrication shop that did custom jobs for special events, parties, movie and game sets, and promotional campaigns. It contained four bots that worked in tandem,[153] each specially programmed for its role on a per-project basis. Currently, one was cutting thick sheet metal in a pumpkin pattern, one was connecting sections of a side steel frame and welding them tight, one was painting the cut sheet metal a garish orange, and one was constructing a wheelbase frame. When completed, it would be one of several self-propelled functional pumpkin carriages used to entertain philanthropic guests at a Cinderella-themed fundraising ball to help impoverished Great American people who were unable to afford their own glass slippers.

The shop was not one of those with a gated path through the factory that allowed self-guided tours while bots worked.

---

[152] Even the ones that did not manufacture timekeeping devices.

[153] Yes, *tandem* traditionally refers to a team of two, not four, but it also can mean a number of people (or bots!) working together. Four, as you know, is a number.

Only the hallway floor-to-ceiling viewing window let us see the work inside. Of course, I could have broken through the window if necessary, but it wasn't. At this distance, I could read the bots and the security vid, which was all we needed, Harken said. My reading wouldn't disturb the bots or their work. In a jiffy we'd have all the vid and bot logs from the day the gigantic bottle was fabricated for Sannien's party. We'd be able to see the surreptitious cutting mechanism being installed, the fabric matching Margoria's dress being planted. We'd have incontrovertible evidence showing General Major Driver or someone working for him was responsible for the bottle falling and the damage it caused. The food court would have to reevaluate Margoria's conviction.

My partner's plan ran into two small obstacles. The first was the strange fact that the bots were missing logs. The three hours it had taken the bots to construct the perfume bottle were not in the bots' records, as if that time had passed without their awareness. I am using *aware* here not to mean *sentient*, which the bots were not, but to mean something more like *detecting activities, movement, and immediate environment.* Bots maintained a log of what they did, where they did it, what other objects or beings were in close [154] proximity while they performed whatever function they were performing. It helped improve processes and protect manufacturers from liability, was crucial for those bots, like betbots and smorgasbots, that directly interacted with humans. Logs were not optional. They weren't supposed to be erased. Yet these bots had apparently been nowhere doing nothing at all at the time the bottle was being put together.

The second obstacle was that the security vid showed no tampering. During the three hours the bots were not logging their activities, they were, according to the vid, busy building the giant bottle of Sannien's Smell. There were no humans in the vid. Not Margoria, not Driver, not anyone. Just the bots. They cut and welded and bolted and lifted, starting with many

---

[154] Distant proximity was generally not relevant.

parts and ending with a finished product, a massive phallic gold bottle of perfume, all of it on vid, none of it edited. What was not on vid, no matter how much it was magnified, was any sign of the cutting mechanism that had been hidden inside the unit. Not only was there no sign of it, but it was positively not there. The vid clearly showed the inside of the unit as the bots assembled it, without even a hint of the device on a pedestal, the one we had seen at the party inside the broken bottle. I summarized my findings and projected the vid on a cinderblock wall so Harken could see for himself.

"Are you sure it isn't there somewhere? Should I watch all three hours of the vid?"

"I'm sure," I told him. It's true—I was.

"Let me understand this. You're telling me that the vid shows no interference by a person, that no person was there at all, and also clearly shows the bots didn't install, that is, the device we know was in the bottle, because we saw it with our own eyes at the party, isn't there. Is that right?"

"I don't have eyes, but otherwise that is accurate. Yet the vid doesn't appear to be altered. I should be able to detect even a deep fake."

"It's obviously fake," he said. "Simple logic tells us that. You've already accessed vid of the bottle being transported, vid of the bottle once it was at OceanLand, right, and there was no interference there?"

"Right."

"Well, the device that cut the bottle and dropped it on my head was there, we know that. And if the bots were not keeping logs, that's when it was installed, no matter what the vid says. Too big of a coincidence otherwise."

"I agree," I said. "But is that evidence?"

"It's evidence," he said.

"Evidence of what?"

"Evidence that someone with serious resources was behind this. Margoria couldn't have faked a vid so completely that even you can't detect it. And how in the world would she have been able to mess with the bots' logs? She's barely staying in business as a ventriloquism teacher. She doesn't have the money to hire someone capable of this."

"And Driver does?"

"Maybe. I don't know. Our evidence doesn't prove he had anything specifically to do with it, but it doesn't have to. This isn't an episode of *Matlock*. We don't have to expose the real perpetrator in court. We just have to show that Margoria couldn't have done it. At the least, the vid and missing logs prove this was a sophisticated operation that warrants more investigation."

I handed Harken some coffee because he had mentioned a twentieth-century television show, which I explained earlier usually meant he needed a boost.

He accepted it with gratitude.

I asked, "Will a food court judge agree?"

"I hope so. For Margoria's sake, I hope so."

We were walking to the food court when Nutella came out of nowhere. Not literally, since some law of physics[155] or philosophy[156] probably applied, but even my sensors didn't pick her up until she arrived.

She told Harken he looked like hell.

"It's been one of those days. You missed a fun trial. A model of Great American jurisprudence."

"I've seen the highlights."

"Can I assume you were listening in on our conversation with Driver in his housing unit?"

---

[155] I'd go into more detail if the math weren't too complicated for most humans to follow.

[156] Descartes believed that something could not arise from nothing, but keep in mind he reached this conclusion without having had the opportunity to read the true accounts of our adventures.

"You can, but only the beginning. It sounded like you smacked him into next week and then we lost the signal. You broke our mic. I might have to bill you for that."

"Put it on my tab."

"So, the bottle was Driver, not Margoria? You're certain?"

Harken told Nutella he was. And he told her about the bots with the missing logs and the vid that showed no tampering with the bottle during construction.

"Erasing bot logs and manipulating vid doesn't sound like something Margoria could do," she said. "Doesn't sound like something Driver could, either, not by himself."

Harken agreed. "Even more so when you add paralyzing Arjay at the precise moment the bottle fell to keep him from helping me. Celeb managers don't usually have that kind of tech."

"And we don't know who messaged GAD to tell us you were going to be killed. If Driver was working alone, how could anyone else have known about it? And why warn us?"

"Right. Something bigger is going on here. One thing I know is Driver's not gonna tell us anything. We have nothing on him."

"That leaves you with a problem."

"What problem?"

"Harken, he tried to kill you and failed. He could try again and have better luck."

"Oh, that. Yeah."

"You might want to do something about it."

"I might. Speaking of someone trying to kill me, if you're able to find out who sent you the anonymous warning, that might help me figure out who Driver's working with."

She said, "We'll keep looking. Meanwhile, I have to head to the Central Region for a different case. What's your plan now?"

"We're going to find the food court judge, show her the vid of bots building a bottle, show her the empty logs, all evidence Margoria wasn't there. Maybe that'll be enough to get a retrial. It should be." He didn't sound convinced.

The food court was not in session. Even justice had to sleep some time. The food part of the food court was still open, of course. It always was. There were people here and there eating danishes or croissants or pizza. One drunk guy who was clearly more there than here was eating all three. Between Scalzi's Bewildering[157] Burritos and Gabino's Tres Tasty Tacos was the oversized, ornate door to the judge's chambers. It was closed and guarded by ten GAS officers. Gunner Claymore was standing in front of them, waiting for us. "I wondered when you'd show up," he said.

Harken responded cleverly with, "Huh? How'd you know we were coming?" I had been blocking the peacegrid to prevent GAS tracking and interference. Claymore couldn't have been watching us.

"I knew you'd be back. When we took Margoria into custody, you told her you'd get her out. I heard you promise. We've been here since the trial to make sure you and that appliance don't interfere with justice."

"Well, tell the judge I have new evidence, vid showing Margoria was nowhere near the bottle at any time during its construction. It's enough for a new trial, at least."

"There won't be any new trial."

Harken said, "That decision's above your paygrade. We'll see what the judge thinks."

"No, we won't."

"Claymore, I don't have time for your games."

"You have all the time in the world. The judge won't be seeing you or any of your so-called evidence and it doesn't matter what your vid shows. Margoria's already been exiled."

My partner was silent at first. It was as if Claymore's words were in some indecipherable language and Harken just stared, turned his head a little like a dog does when it seems to be trying

---

[157] And possibly ill-advised.

to understand what a person is saying. Finally, he said, "Exiled?"

"Yes, exiled."

"I was gone for an hour."

Claymore sneered. "You should be faster next time."

Harken rushed at Claymore, was grabbed by three officers before he could lay a hand on him. They struggled to hold him as he reached for their chief. The other seven officers had stunners aimed and ready. Harken yelled, "I asked you to take it slow, to buy me a little time! All you had to do was process the arrest like any other arrest! No one has a trial so fast! No one gets exiled so fast!"

Claymore was enjoying himself. "I don't work for you, you two-bit wannabe. I'm gonna let this attempted assault go, won't throw you in a cell, only because I'm feeling generous. You'll walk away now if you don't want a stay at a GAS station."

I hadn't moved the entire time. I might have been able to take out Claymore and the rest of the officers, but Harken would probably be stunned in the process. My calculations indicated that taking action was more rather than less likely to lead to harm to Harken, if not in the moment, then later. The case was over. Margoria had been exiled. There was no point to fighting now.

Harken still reached for Claymore, just a few seconds more, then let up. All the energy seemed to drain from his body. The officers held him until Claymore was satisfied Harken had settled down and then Harken was released. I followed as without a word he turned away from the GAS officers and walked through the food court, pausing only to kick over an empty chair at a table.

To say that he was still angry would be an understatement, a kind of statement I generally avoid. But he appeared to realize that as much as he'd yelled at Claymore for the rushed trial, GAS officers weren't in charge of food courts. This went higher, at least as high as the judge, maybe higher. In any case, as mad as he was at the Great American judicial system, he knew the real person to blame for Margoria's exile didn't work at the food court.

His redirected anger grew as we walked. "You recorded our conversation upstairs with Driver?"

"Yes," I said.

"Can you edit it?"

"Of course."

"And you were blocking other vid devices in his housing unit? Yours is the only recording?"

"Yes. I blocked all vid when you told me to open his door and I disabled GAD's recording device when you hit Driver. I didn't think we wanted anyone listening in."

"Good," Harken said, still angry but now also suddenly calm, having reached a decision.

20

Win-Fall wasn't as crowded as the last time we'd visited, during our first case. It was much later at night this time and even Great Americans had to sleep eventually. Still, there were plenty of people playing blackjack, pulling handles at slot machines, cheering at the roulette arena for the person running in a giant hamster ball to land on red. At Argumania, the argumatons were vigorously debating whether or not a hot dog is a sandwich[158] while spectators wagered and drank. In unrelated food news, the buffet had removed heavy dinner options and replaced them with snacks and desserts. Soon it would be time to bring out breakfast selections for early risers.

Harken told the two sport-coat guys guarding the door at the private backroom that we needed to talk to Tommy Ten-Toes. The backroom's broken glass coffee table and cue sticks had been replaced with nonbroken ones. There was no evidence

---

[158] It is not.

of the violence the room had seen eight days earlier. Iceberg stood on burgundy carpet next to the billiards table, his white tuxedo still immaculate. His face didn't hide his displeasure with us for ditching him when he'd gone to the bathroom, and Harken's face didn't hide his not-caring-even-a-little-about-Iceberg's-displeasure.

Ten-Toes entered the private backroom from another even more private backroom at the back of the private backroom. Technically, it was a backbackroom. "Detective Harken, to what do I owe this honor?"

"You wanted a name, I have a name."

"What're you talking about? Margoria's already been exiled." News traveled fast in the Great American, especially if you had a network of omnipresent gluten dealers.

"I know," Harken said, making no effort to hide his bitterness. "She's innocent."

"It really wasn't Margoria?"

"It really wasn't Margoria. Someone else caused that bottle to fall, put Sannien's life at risk, for personal gain."

"How do you know?"

"Ten-Toes, I'm a detective. Knowing is what I do. Do you want the name or not?"

"I do."

Harken handed him the folded-up sign he'd saved from the Treeseeum. He'd deleted the flashing words *These Are Clues* and replaced them with three other words, the name of the person responsible for much of today's misery. The person whose vendetta and greed had caused Sannien to lose a tail and Margoria to be exiled.

Ten-Toes looked at the name on the sign. "Driver?"

"That's right."

"Why would Driver want to kill Sannien?"

"He wasn't trying to kill Sannien. He was trying to kill *me*—an old grudge from outside. Sannien got caught in the crossfire because Driver planned for it to happen at the party, wanted witnesses, so he could frame Margoria and keep her from interfering with Sannien's relationship with The Juggler. He was willing to risk Sannien being hurt to be sure he kept his new client."

"You're saying my marketing plan lost a tail because Driver wanted to frame a ventriloquist?"

"Pretty much," Harken said.

"You have evidence?"

"I do. Arjay?"

That was my cue. I played the audio from our conversation with General Major Driver:

HARKEN
You put that fabric in the bottle to frame Margoria for a little money. Tell the truth.

DRIVER
If you've seen The Juggler's act, you know it was for a lot of money. You said yourself he's going to be big, bigger than Sannien. I admit I did it.

My editing was as superb as my coffee.[159] I had modified inflection so the words fit perfectly where placed, sounded as natural as could be—no one would be able to tell my version wasn't the actual conversation exactly as it had happened.

Harken told me to give Ten-Toes the audio drive, so I did.

"Go ahead, have it tested. It's authentic," Harken said.

Ten-Toes took the drive. "Do I want to know what you did to make him confess?"

"Nothing you wouldn't do."

Ten-Toes couldn't argue with that. Whatever it was, he'd done worse to get answers from people.

Before turning to leave, Harken said, "You wanted a name, I gave you a name. What you do with it is none of my business."

---

[159] This is hyperbole, of course. My editing was flawless, but my coffee was better than that.

Ten-Toes didn't respond, just said to himself in a low voice, "Driver." He didn't sound mad because he rarely does. He did sound deadly serious, though. "Driver!"

We headed out of Win-Fall as he called over a couple of sport coats to give orders. He was no longer the feared crime boss he'd been on the outside, was now a mild-mannered and peaceful entertainment mogul. A legitimate businessperson. Yet, as Driver would find out, it was still a very bad idea to cross Tommy Ten-Toes.

Frank Harken's housing unit always welcomed him home with music, and this time it was Cannonball Adderley's "Somethin' Else." He shut it off.

"That was a strange case," I said. "Aren't we supposed to save the day? We figured out the truth about the blackmailer, but I expected us to prevent Margoria from being exiled, too."

"I expected the same thing."

"It doesn't seem fair," I said.

"No, it doesn't."

"It's only my eighth day being a detective. Will this be how cases usually end?"

"I don't know if there is *usually* anymore. We don't always get what we expect."

"Was changing Driver's audio good detective work? I know he tried to kill you and framed Margoria, but I didn't think we were supposed to make our own evidence like that."

"No, it wasn't good detective work. It wasn't good at all. You're right, we're not supposed to—it's not something I've ever done before."

"Is it ironic that we fabricated evidence against someone who fabricated evidence?"

He barely shrugged. "I don't know."[160]

"We're still the good guys, though, right?"

---

[160] He was a detective, not an English professor.

I might have detected a slight nod.

In all my eight days, I'd never seen Harken so down. I tried to cheer him up with my unbridled[161] optimism. "The day could have been worse. At least you're not dead."

"At least I'm not dead," he said, though he didn't sound very enthusiastic about it.

Then he saw the small, wrapped box on the floor, delivered while we were still at Win-Fall talking with Ten-Toes. "What's this?"

"A gift."

"From you?"

"Yes. I felt bad about getting you a hat you didn't like and keeping it for myself. You deserve better on our eight-day-iversary."

"What is it?"

"You have to open it to find out. That's how gifts work."

"Arjay, I've had a really crappy day. And do you know how tired I am?"

"I do, only theoretically, based on calculations. I don't get tired and have no practical experience. Open your gift!"

Harken was too tired to argue and unwrapped the box. Inside was a watch. "It's a watch," he said.

"Not just any watch. This is top-of-the-line, cutting-edge technology. You can communicate with me, connect with others, watch shows, shop for a new hat, it does so much."

"Does it tell time?"

"Yes."

"Can I turn off all the other stuff?"

"Yes."

"Then I'll keep it." He paused, then said, "Thank you for the gift. It's very thoughtful."

I agreed. "Yes, it is."

"Give me a minute." Harken went into the other room and came back out forty-eight seconds later, which is less than a minute.

---

[161] Horses!

He handed me a smooth pebble, 1.953 inches across, nearly transparent quartz. "Happy eight-day-iversary."

"It's a smooth pebble," I said.

"Yes. It's a smooth pebble. This is from a beach back east. I collected them when I was a kid on the outside. I said if you did well today maybe you'd get a pet rock. You did better than well today, partner, even if it didn't all work out like we wanted it to."

Technically, quartz was a rock-forming mineral, but that didn't mean it couldn't also be a pet rock. "I will name it Pebbly."

"You do that. I'm going to bed." Maybe sleep would bring him some peace, though the odds were against it.

And Frank Harken went to bed, leaving me alone with Pebbly the pet rock. It was instantly my favorite possession I'd ever possessed—I loved Pebbly even more than my dear departed hat. As I powered down for what little remained of the night, I gripped the flawless emblem of our rock-solid part-nership and promised to keep it forever.

ACKNOWLEDGEMENTS

Thank you to Andee Stein, Chris Matarazzo, Van McCourt-Ostrand, Gail Rosen, Albert DiBartolomeo, and Amy Boshnack for reading early drafts and providing encouragement.

Thank you to Galen Surlak-Ramsey and Jenn Wallace for exceptional editorial advice and for pushing me to make this book better.

Thank you to Andrew Turner for valuable feedback about the cover design. Thank you to Jodi Goldstein for providing the coffee mug and hand illustrations for the book's interior.

Thank you to Gabe Hudson, Vikram Paralkar, Mike Sacks, and Chantel Acevedo for generous and enthusiastic blurbs.

Thank you to all the readers who enjoyed the first book and to everyone who recommended it to others. I hope you like this one, too.

Thank you to Andee, Griffin, and Buster for everything.

ABOUT THE AUTHOR

Photo Credit: Joel Kaufman

Scott Stein is the author of four novels: *The Great American Betrayal, The Great American Deception, Mean Martin Manning,* and *Lost*.

His writing has appeared in *The Oxford University Press Humor Reader, McSweeney's, Philadelphia Inquirer, National Review, Reason, Art Times, Liberty, The G.W. Review, Points in Case,* and *New York* magazine.

He is a professor of English at Drexel University.

Website: scottsteinonline.com
Twitter: @sstein

ABOUT THE PUBLISHER

Tiny Fox Press LLC
5020 Kingsley Road
North Port, FL 34287

www.tinyfoxpress.com

CPSIA information can be obtained
at www.ICGtesting.com
Printed in the USA
BVHW041448270922
648086BV00006B/172